Small Town Memories

A CLEAN SMALL TOWN ROMANCE COLLECTION

MAPLEWOOD GROVE
BOOK TWO

DAISY LANDISH

Editing by Jessica McKenna
Cover by Daisy Landish

Sweet Winter

A SMALL TOWN SECOND CHANCE ROMANCE

Chapter One

SAM

ALL FIVE MEMBERS of Pearl Jam smolder at him from the poster stuck to the unremarkable white wall of his childhood bedroom.

This, Sam thinks, is a telling snapshot of his life these days: lying akimbo in a bed his feet hang off of whenever he slides too far down his pillow, and a band he hasn't listened to in years looking down at him with reproach.

He almost feels guilty. He almost feels guilty a lot these days. It's the kind of guilt that's becoming somewhat signature to him. A brand of it that he has too much pride to commit to fully, yet not enough self-involved arrogance to pull off.

"*SAMMY! BREAKFAST!*" his mom yells from downstairs. Like she sensed his eyes opening. Or she thinks he's slept in enough. He pats around the mattress for his phone, lost in the folds of his polka-dotted quilt. *Yeah, 8 AM. Slept in enough.* His train of thought reeks of sardonicism these days.

He opts for a meditative exhale. It comes out a resigned sigh. Lying in bed will only make this general ennui worse. He's discovered that a record-breaking three days into being back in Maplewood Grove. His hometown. The same one he'd run from as soon as he could... and left plenty behind in, almost everything but a single duffle bag full of clothing he'd grown out of within the first year of college. He hadn't meant to run. He'd just been looking for something that didn't exist in this small town.

He's still looking, he thinks. Forty-three years old, and feeling painfully seventeen.

Almost twenty-five years later, he remembers how he'd thought: *Weddings or funerals are all I'll come back for.* The kind of passive-aggressive, flippant promises of someone young enough to think they knew everything.

Weddings or funerals, he'd thought.

Now, it's too close a call to the latter that's yanked him back here.

Back to the same bathroom that they'd all shared, fighting to get dressed in the mornings. Sam almost expects to see his lanky teenage self in the mirror. Instead, while he brushes the sourness out of his mouth, the darkened bags under his eyes screech Middle-Aged Adult. "It doesn't have to be forever," he tells his reflection, spraying foamy spittle every which way. The traitorous greys creeping into the shadow of stubble across his jaw mocks him.

"*SAMMY!*" his mom's voice cuts through the reverie.

Sam scrunches his eyes shut, spitting into the sink. "*Coming, Ma!*" he finally hollers back. He wipes his mouth, and the mirror, then makes his way downstairs.

He pretends the faces in the photographs that line the stairwell wall don't glare at him with every step he descends. It isn't hard. Three days of practice is enough to nail it.

Unfortunately, the same cannot be said for the shrewd look on the face of the man at the breakfast table with his hand already wrapped around a mug of coffee. He's in his police uniform. Very distinguished, and he definitely knows it. What's eeriest is how much like Sam himself he looks – only, obviously better.

"Don't you have a house of your own?" Sam asks his brother.

Solomon Walker is the elder of the two Walker children. Sam's big brother by four and a half years. And he never lets Sam forget it. Sam can hear the way his own voice grows pinched with irritation, the longer they face off.

In a way, they have always been this way. *Natural,* their dad calls it. In another, it's this: "It doesn't need to be *my house* to be my family," Sol says. *My.* Not *our.* Sam doesn't miss it. He isn't supposed to. It's a minor miracle his teeth don't audibly grind. "Just a part of my routine. Checking in after dropping the kiddos off at school. Has been since after Pop's stroke, Sammy. You'd know if you'd been here." *There it is.*

The taunt isn't new. It isn't even a taunt, coming from his brother. That's not Sol. No, Sol is never that juvenile. That's a role better assigned to him. Sol is the Reasonable One. The one with the answers. The good son, the one who stayed. It had been him who'd made the call to Sam last week when their father had collapsed in the grocery store. Sam wishes he were a big enough person for that to not chafe at him, but he's not.

"I'm here now," Sam says curtly.

"Sure. In your pajamas all day. Skulking around uselessly."

He wishes he wouldn't flinch. That there wouldn't be the petulant edge to his voice when he demands, "What's your point, man?"

Sol doesn't pause. Like he'd been waiting for Sam to ask, he answers without hitch, "Just because you're back in our small town doesn't mean you've got to treat it like you're slumming it. My point is, if you're here then *be here.*"

Sam snorts his derision. "And how the heck would you have me do that?"

"Figure it out, Peter Pan," Sol says. "Be a man for once in your life."

Next to the beat-up Jeep his dad's had since Sam was a kid, his glossy BMW looks out of place. Sam doesn't bother getting into it when he steps out of the house. Everything his brother had said felt unfair. This didn't mean it was likely it was a shared sentiment around town.

It is roughly 9 AM. He'd managed to get showered and dressed after his brother landed a few more kicks at his downtrodden pride. Sam is already out of fight for the day. Maybe for the week. He'd have to check his reserves again at the end of the day – on the off chance that something just might fill his cup.

He takes off on foot. Whether he's now perceived as an outsider, or the Maplewood Grove native he is for better and for worse, Sam hasn't forgotten how this place works. He gets a little thrill out of eliciting a look of pleasant astonishment out of more than one passer-by when he greets them by name as he jaunts through town.

It's almost enough for him to forget he doesn't have a destination in mind. Not as much as he has a mental list of destinations he won't go. The top of which is likely to feature the most morning traffic: Loretta's Diner. A classic American diner with delicious dishes and more town gossip than the newsstand down the street. Sam can't help but think of it like a fishbowl.

Maybe he was being presumptuous. Maybe Sol had made him paranoid. There was always that chance. But he *wasn't* Peter Pan; contrary to his brother's reviews, he wasn't always up to taking a chance.

Besides, it wasn't as if Maplewood Grove was prone to change. The same sidewalks and same shops line the streets. Even the décor that's begun to bedeck the town is somewhat recycled from previous years. He can tell. He recognizes the lights strung up between street light poles. Of course, the town is still buzzing with excitement.

Fortunately, Sam doesn't have to go far to get answers. He asks the first person he sees: Cliff Barnett. The grizzly owner of the Sip 'n Saw bar could come off as intimidating—but he'd only been a couple of years ahead of Sam in school. Asking, "What's with the—?" while gesturing vaguely at the banners strung up down the street featuring a couple of aged men who looked familiar but not.

"Heritage Festival," Cliff replies after a brusque nod in greeting. "They're doing a theme for the winter festival this year."

Sam almost laughs, raising a hand in thanks as Cliff carries on past him. He wasn't expecting the man to stop to exchange idle pleasantries. He'd bet the bar owner didn't even need to ask why Sam was in town. There were chances most people in this town had known about his dad's stroke before he had. If he'd asked Sam what he was doing, what would he even answer? He looks at Cliff's retreating back, watching him until he's turned the corner and out of sight.

Yeah, he thinks, *probably best he didn't stop.*

MAGGIE

A couple of streets over, Loretta's Diner is precisely where a bespectacled brunette walks into. She wouldn't necessarily call herself a casual frequenter. A woman couldn't afford to eat out so often with a librarian's paycheck, after all. She's definitely not here for the gossip.

But Maggie Foster did like her little routines.

Especially on days like today, the ones where she felt like a storm cloud was following her around. She calls them her Blue Days. It's her favorite color and makes them sound less insidious than they feel. The days when there is just something in the air that coats her skin in a film negativity sticks to, like a fly in honey.

She prides herself in not letting even these get her down. It may not be easy. But Maggie is a methodical woman. She knows when not to be alone with herself. Of course, she respects herself too much to force herself to talk to anyone either, when she's not much of a conversational partner to dance around with.

Her solution, therefore, is tried and true: the diner.

Where conversation always formlessly hums around her without needing her input or intervention. It just *is.* That's comforting to her. She breathes a little easier just opening the door.

Immediately upon stepping in from the January chill, Maggie spots a familiar head of golden hair. Her friend and fellow Book Club bluestocking, Rachel Green, is herding her little boy out of the diner bathroom. From the way Rachel dabs at Jamie's pudgy little hands, Maggie deduces they're done eating and on their way out.

Only a beat later, Rachel spots her back. She waves with an exhausted sort of enthusiasm that's become signature to her. "Maggie!" Rachel huffs, taking a break from grinning at her to glare at her son until he lets her wrap a cozy green scarf around his neck. "Gosh, I wish I'd known you were coming in. Breakfast with a real adult conversation may have been just the thing. I'm—Well, you know."

Maggie smiles softly at her. She does know. Rachel, new in town and still finding roots to put down, has been on the hunt for a job. No luck yet. She doubts the little boy shyly looking at her from where he's tucked himself by Rachel's hip does, though, so she stays mum. Her dark blond hair conceals the greys a closer look would pinpoint.

She squeezes Rachel's hand in passing. "Good luck. I've got my fingers crossed for you," Maggie promises, then holds her hand up to show her how literally she means it. Just in case Rachel needs it.

"Thanks, Mags," the woman says warmly. "I'll see ya later, right?"

It isn't long after Maggie agrees that Rachel's gone.

The exchange is brief. Not at all unwelcome. But when Maggie drops down into the closest chair, she does so heavily. Jasmine, one of the kids Loretta lets waitress before school some days, takes her order —"*A plate of some of that fluffy French toast with a cup of hot chocolate!*"—after a swift greeting, takes it to the kitchen, and then she's on her way out the door too. She doesn't instigate the regular exchange of pleasantries and only leaves with a friendly wave.

Maggie releases a relieved breath. So far, the universe is on her side, it seems.

She is free to take her time laying that week's *Maplewood Grove Gazette* out in front of her, paging her way to the crossword puzzle. She's barely four words into solving it when that warm egg and sugar smell envelops her, making her mouth water. Loretta Beam, owner and namesake of this diner that's always been here, sets her plate and mug down in front of her. "Enjoy, sweets," Loretta coos, squeezing Maggie's shoulder on her way back behind the counter.

She sets down her pencil to pick up a knife and fork. The toast is still visibly too hot, but she can't help it. Maggie is huffing with her ruddy cheeks puffed like a blowfish, exhaling steam and regretting her burnt tongue, when she hears a familiar pair of voices behind her.

Well, she hears *tutting* at first. Then, she hears, "So unfortunate. In her 40s and not one prospect—" A second, similar voice intersects, intertwining, "How could there be? That gal blinks at anyone who dares to look her way until they run for the hills!" It's the Carlton twins. Maggie can rarely, if ever, tell the two apart. It isn't anywhere near as difficult to decipher who the subject of their exchange is, though. "Living her life away in books..." the first voice adds as if Maggie needed any confirmation to know it's her they're talking about.

She lets out a slow, tempering breath.

If it works, Maggie doesn't find out. One of the twins audibly grumbles, "Ah, she didn't even come to the last meeting, did you know?" It is the other's turn to cluck her tongue like a disapproving hen. Maggie's stomach turns. She can see the hand around her fork quivering.

"If she had, she would've heard what Gene said."

Gene... Maggie considers. *The mayor. What—?*

"Poor girl. What's she gonna have left when they have to shut the library down?" Maggie's terror ratchets. Her utensils drop with a clatter. She doesn't hear the aged twins' reaction to that; her blood roars in her ears too loudly, flowing in a panicked rush. The sugar turns sour in her mouth.

She's going to be sick. She would be, right now, if she had more than half a bite of French toast in her system. Even that may just fall out of the hole that's been burrowed in her chest. It feels that way. Like she's been stabbed through the chest with an icicle from outside. Like the two old women have conspired to bundle a fistful of snow, and then shot it right at her face like a fastball.

With bones filled with lead, Maggie somehow scrambles to her feet. Some part of her brain must remember where she is and what she is doing; even in her stricken haste, she pulls out a handful of cash and leaves it on the table beside a meal she cannot see through blurring vision. Maggie runs.

Even the snow crunching beneath her boots outside goes, *Oh no, oh no, oh no.*

She didn't have to think about where to go. There's only ever one real option. This, in hindsight, is where she should've just come in the first place. This library is her haven. Maggie may have a small, unremarkable, but inherited house. But it's this building where she feels grounded. Here, where she feels more corporeal.

Here, her panic feels far away. Just an ephemeral infection she's left on the other side of the heavy oak doors. *Yeah,* Maggie thinks to herself, ruffling her bangs out of her eyes as she puts another selection of recently dusted hardbacks away.

She isn't sure how long she's necessarily been at it. All that matters is how steady her hands are as she systemically makes her way through the aisles. These aisles she could make her way through in the dark. That's how much history she has here. She loved it before she ever worked here. It's been hers longer than she's had a badge to prove it. When she's surrounded by it, it doesn't feel like something to be ashamed of. What the doddering Carlton twins had said felt like facts, not censure.

Maggie is forty-two years old. She doesn't have romantic prospects. She doesn't feign interest in any. She does live her life surrounded by books. She can live her life that way, it feels good to her.

So what if it sometimes felt like it was all she had? Surely, it was better than having nothing. This is her life. It didn't happen to her by accident. A series of choices she can't find herself regretting had resulted in it. It's her life, and it's mostly quiet nights alone and places where bitterness made her harder years ago—but it's fine.

When she's got her fingers wrapped around the solid metal handle of the cart, and the comforting, familiar creak of the wheels every time she moves them, it isn't hard to ignore the stagnant feeling in her stomach.

It isn't as effortless to dismiss the way her stomach comes to life when confronted with the sight around the corner. The back of a curly head of hair that's only dark enough to escape being blond by a single shade. Oh, Maggie's breath shallows. *Oh.* Her stomach somersaults. It isn't a ghost, is it? No.

A slight turn—and his profile is in view, just like that.

Maggie would know Samuel Everett Walker anywhere.

As if he feels her too, he turns to face her. Maggie doesn't have enough functioning brain cells to fathom the implications of that. It takes a moment too long for recognition to dawn on his face. Her chest aches all over again. If the Carlton twins had plummeted a snowball at her face, Sam aims one right at her sternum. It's a miracle she doesn't keel over.

But she's a strong woman. She absorbs the look on his face and remembers it all. Hadn't he once been such a monumental part of her figuring that out?

Maggie wonders if this is a reminder from the universe: *You survived him. You could survive this loss, too – if it comes down to it.* She only realizes how she's been staring, for how long, when he pierces her reverie. He clears his throat. Maggie startles, flinching with her whole body.

"Hi, Mag—" he starts. Maggie feels her face shutter. *No,* she thinks. No. Never again. Not a chance. She isn't interested. Not ever again.

The wheels of her cart screech over the sharp turn she demands of them. "If there's anything I can help you with, please let me know," she says brusquely, walking away from him. Mechanically. Like he's a stranger.

Hadn't it been his choice for that to be all they are today?

Chapter Two

MAGGIE

"MAGGIE? YOU OKAY?" Isabel's rich, rumbling voice jars her out of her haze.

A *haze* is probably an understatement. Maggie had fallen down a rabbit hole—tripped into one, actually, and she can't seem to stop falling. She's been falling all day. If any one of the women in this room were to ask her how she'd gotten from the library that morning to her seat in their circle at the Whispering Willow, Maggie knows she wouldn't have an answer.

As it is, she doesn't even know where to begin answering Isabel Martinez's question. If it occurred to her to lie, she wouldn't be able to pull it off. Maggie didn't practice lying enough, and Isabel had too much practice being shrewd. The woman, albeit younger than Maggie by a handful of years, maintains a gently intimidating aura, even with those warm brown eyes affixed to Maggie now. Maggie opens her mouth. Then closes it again.

"Cool it, Iz," Rachel interjects, saving her, moving from her seat to crouch by Maggie's side. Her hand pets through Maggie's hair. Maggie wonders if her son knows how lucky he is, to be raised by someone to whom love comes so easily. Rachel asks softly, the same question: "*Are* you okay, though?"

Maggie doesn't think about it. She just shakes her head. "I don't think so," she answers. "Not at all."

"Say more," Diana Hayes prompts with a familiar refrain. She's younger than all of the rest of them—but somehow, past the youthful features that betrayed her age in the 20s, she is anything but immature. She just may be the best listener Maggie has ever met; she's got the habit of only speaking when she's got something important to add. Somehow, she still can't ever be accused of being inattentive.

These three women don't know everything about her. But they do know her. They know her in a way that supersedes facts and judgments. Instead, they know the way she perceives the world. How she thinks about life, treachery, and love, about fantastical creatures and the most flawed of human beings. One path of knowledge has a broader scope; the other is deeper. It is anything but insignificant to Maggie, that she feels safe enough to tell them.

"Do you ever," she begins, "wake up with a pit in your stomach? Almost like you're holding a breath you can't let go?"

"Waiting for the other shoe to drop?" Isabel checks. "Oh yes."

Rachel giggles. "I'm a single mom, Mags. I live in that place."

Maggie offers a watery smile in return. "Well, I can deal with that feeling, usually. Today, however, it just—it did. The shoe. It dropped."

Now, Diana guesses, "The budget cuts Mayor Beckett brought up at the last town meeting." Maggie gives a shaky, grateful nod her way. "He said he was concerned, not that it was final. Has something changed?" Diana is every inch a journalist. Her questions are direct, harboring no nonsense.

Maggie can't help but answer earnestly, "I don't know, Diana. I don't—I don't love the meetings, you guys know that. I didn't go. The Carlton twins broke it to me this morning—"

"—*suuuper* gently, I'm sure," Isabel mutters sarcastically.

Despite herself, Maggie snuffles a light laugh. "Very, yes. Um. While reeling from that, I ran into an ex between the library shelves."

"*You have an ex?!*" Rachel nearly screeches, every syllable soaked in astonishment.

Maggie's face heats. Resigned, she confirms, "Sam Walker. He's... Yeah. He's... You could say he is *the* ex." Her breath is shaky. She barrels forward quickly, insistent. "I don't care. I don't—I don't want to care, at least. I don't have time to care, and I'm definitely not going to waste any more on that man than I already did. I'm more stressed out about the library. I need to figure out a way to come up with a way to save it."

Diana only looks at her, quiet and calculating. It's unnerving. Isabel shatters the tension like glass, announcing with gusto, "Then let's come up with a solution." She punctuates slapping her hardback shut forcefully. No arguments to be brooked.

<hr />

Maggie had forgotten her own capacity when confronted by the re-emergence of a ghost from her past. By the next evening, on the other side of a fervent talking-to from the women she admired most, that same haunting has been reshaped into a bucket full of gumption.

It fuels her enough to not just get her to a town meeting but to call an emergency, after-hours one herself. As it turned out, when one put four heads together, a solution simply couldn't be that far behind. It made mathematical sense, Rachel had ventured. What chance did *one* problem stand against *four* of them?

As she walks up to the podium they brought up to the makeshift stage in the corner of the Sip 'n Saw bar, Maggie is inclined to agree.

Especially armed with notes outlining her strategy in her hand. She doesn't need them. The girls helped her prepare and practice the speech enough times, she could give it in her sleep. Still, it soothes her nerves to have them.

"Hi, guys," she greets sheepishly and adjusts her glasses at the bridge of her nose. "As I'm sure you've heard—" Maggie stares pointedly at the Carlton twins, always sat right in the front row, hands on their hearing aids just so they didn't miss a thing, "—the mayor has been struggling with budget after looking at annual projections. And, as I'm sure you'll all agree, the library is a centerpiece of town history. Which happens to be exactly what we're celebrating this winter festival.

"Now, we also have a meteor shower coming up. A couple of years ago, I'm sure some of you remember, some of us at the library helped raise money to get a telescope in the library. My suggestion is to integrate that into the festival. Just, imagine with me here: What if we walked through our beautiful town with handmade luminaries, while our very own Dot leads whoever buys a ticket with a real-time history lesson on the luminaries who've made this town what it is?" With a sweeping gesture, just like Isabel had taught her, Maggie signals to Dot. The woman, wrapped in the arms of the bar's owner, waves lightly when many begin to turn in their seats to spot her. "Dot's already agreed. She understands how important this is—not just to me, though it will mean the world to me, but for the whole town. What do you all say?"

For a terrifying second, there is silence. Quiet enough to hear a pin drop.

A silence that is subsequently fissured by the erratic, enthusiastic applause of none other than Mayor Gene Beckett himself. The stout, jolly-faced man bumbles forward, clapping his palms together, exclaiming, "Very good, *very* good, Miss Foster! Revolutionary thinking! Taking charge!" Maggie is so surprised, her face doesn't know what to do with itself. She really doesn't know what to do when he adds, "Marvelous! It should be the *center* of the event, I say!"

As the applause begins to ripple through the crowd, Maggie allows herself a brief moment to imagine the full scope of the festival. It wouldn't just be the luminary walk lighting up the town. The Winter Heritage Festival would become a true celebration of Maplewood Grove's history and traditions. She pictured the ice-sculpting competitions that had been a staple for generations, where local artists transformed blocks of ice into glittering masterpieces under the winter sky. There would be stalls showcasing traditional crafts— handmade quilts, wood carvings, and candles, all crafted by the talented hands of Maplewood Grove's artisans. In the town square, a storytelling circle would gather, with the town's elders recounting legends of old, ensuring that the history of Maplewood Grove wasn't just remembered, but lived, through the people who called it home. This festival, Maggie realized, wasn't just about raising funds for the library—it was about bringing the entire town together to celebrate who they were and where they came from.

In hindsight, perhaps Maggie would realize that calling out the Carlton twins so boldly wasn't her wisest move. It seemed, as she would soon learn, like opening the floodgates to their inevitable meddling. One of them suggests, voice dripping saccharine, "Why doesn't Miss Foster chair the committee? It's her idea, she *should*."

The other chips in, "*Alone?* No, no, Mabel," she clucks, "Miss Foster has a job. *Surely* someone must help her?"

"They must, Agnes, correct! How about—?"

One pretends to consider it. Neither has much of a potential career as an actress, that is to be certain. "How about *Sam Walker?*"

"Agnes! What an *idea!* Ah, yes!"

"You're not doing anything are you, now, Mr. Walker? You said only this morning that you'd *love* to help with the festival ... Building things, you mentioned? He's an architect, you know, Eugene!"

Mayor Beckett, it seems, cannot read the room. Or the look on

Maggie's face, which she would venture must be one of nausea-inducing panic. He begins to clap once more, cheering, "Yes, yes! The community coming together! Spectacular!"

Sharing a transparently sly, conspiratorial glance, the Carlton twins sing-song in eerie tandem: "*They should organize an entire exhibition!*" Maggie's damp palms moisten the edges of her useless notes.

SAM

Whatever descriptors Sam might choose to employ for this week, he couldn't call it boring.

He probably should've known that when his brother had commended, "Your ex-girlfriend called this meeting. Very grown up of you to show up." Sol's compliment had been how Sam had found out. He couldn't very well leave after that, could he?

For a moment in time, once Maggie Foster took the stage, he was glad he hadn't. Seeing her that way, so different from the cold and curt woman he'd run into at the library, she looked like the girl he had once loved. She spoke with singular attention about her beloved library. No one listening could deny her passion for it. None who could argue her adamant belief in the building's importance to the town's cultural identity. Emotion made her come alive.

If Sam had any doubts whatsoever about how the woman felt about him all these years later, they were obliterated the instant the wily old Carlton dames said his name. Maggie's face hardens to stone.

So swiftly, he's left reeling.

The girl he had just gotten to remembering turned back to a mirage. In a way Sam has been careful not to succumb to in all the years between them, he yearnfully remembers her warm eyes, the color of the chocolate she had been borderline addicted to. He had never met someone so easy to please, before Maggie Foster or since. A chocolate bar snuck into her backpack and between one of her books is all it took to make the sun rise on her face. However deceptively plain-looking she may have been otherwise, the minute Maggie smiled, she had the kind of beauty you couldn't look away from.

He must lose himself in remembrance. When he comes to, the townsfolk have already begun to filter out of Cliff's bar—and the woman making her way over to him has eyes he can only describe as *stony*. Her aura, painfully frigid.

At least this time she lets him get out the full, "Hi, Maggie."

She even responds, albeit stiffly, "Hello, Sam."

He only just manages to not succumb to the sudden urge to fuss with his collar. With the way she looks at him—or *through* him, rather—makes him squirm in ways Sam isn't prone to squirming. He attempts levity, joking, "What're the chance, huh," only to have her blink at him, unimpressed.

"Right," she says with finality, once she's decided he's finished. "Look, I don't know what you're playing at here. But you should know this matters to me. I'm not playing a game. My job, at a place I love very much, is at stake here. Why don't you just– Why don't you come to the library tomorrow? We can—"

"I'm in, Maggie. I swear. I'm not messing around here. I really do want to help. In whatever way you'll let me." The words rush out of his mouth of their own volition. All it results in is her looking visibly pained. Sam shoves his hands into his pockets for lack of anything better to do with them.

"I guess we can make a plan," she allows shortly.

Silently, too weary to say anything else, Sam shrugs.

It is enough for Maggie to turn on her heel. Sam only just manages to fully exhale, before she's whipping around again. He could swear he reads indecision in those features, at once familiar and strange to him.

Except then she says, "Sam." Just his name. His heart sinks. "If you could do me the small mercy of just letting this be what it is? I... didn't think I would ever have to see you again. Obviously. So. Once we've saved the library, if you're still around... I will make a concentrated effort to not see you as often as I can. I'd appreciate it if you'd extend me the same courtesy."

He conveys a terse nod he suspects she doesn't even see, with how quickly she escapes. The whole time, he feels like his joints have been frozen stiff.

Chapter Three

SAM

ANOTHER DAY BRINGS along with it a fresh bout of perspective.

Fine, maybe he'd almost talked himself out of showing up to meet someone who obviously wanted nothing to do with him on his way back from the town meeting. But all it took was returning to the time capsule of his childhood bedroom to change his mind.

Sam hadn't meant to linger. But his eyes had sought out the makeshift collage still stuck to the wall above his desk. There was no denying the brunette features in most of them. Her hair may have been bushier and her features softer. It was still Maggie though. Maggie who had been the center of his little universe once upon a time. The same Maggie who he had hurt. He knew he had. And the guilt had never truly left him, no matter how hard he'd tried to bury it under layers of new experiences, new relationships, and the bustling chaos of city life. But none of it—none of it—had ever come close to filling the hollow space she left behind. He had thought time would heal the wounds, but now, standing here, staring at a younger version of her, Sam felt the sharp sting of regret all over again. He couldn't shake the sense that he had abandoned the one person who truly understood him, and the thought haunted him.

He'd always been good at compartmentalizing his emotions. Those compartments were neatly sorted, though. It didn't take much scavenging to unearth an avalanche of guilt from years ago. That was more than enough of a reminder that he really, really couldn't blame Maggie Foster for hating his guts.

Amidst that scavenging, he'd unearthed some core memories of her, too. Enough to suspect he's gotten it right when he does show up at the library the next morning—with a cup of hot chocolate in hand. He can see it all over her face, the moment he holds out the to-go cup: she struggles to make it to the ire she had been planning on.

In the end, Maggie accepts it. Grudging, but polite. "I've—" She gestures vaguely, quick to segue past the matter. Of course, there is plenty of material to distract him. On the long table that she leads him to at the back of the library, she already has a spread going. Upon closer inspection, Sam notes it is littered with old newspapers and article clippings, some photographs too, from what he eventually identifies as material from past winter carnivals in Maplewood Grove.

"Woah. *Wow,*" bursts from Sam's mouth. He risks a glance Maggie's way. But she almost looks bashful at his compliment, and fortunately not irritated by it. That turns him brave enough to ask, "How long have you been at this already?" A quick look at his watch says it's barely past 9 AM.

"A few hours. I couldn't sleep."

He'd almost forgotten how tireless she could be about the things she cared about. He should have known. He had been at the top of that list, once. Maggie had always been a quieter person; he'd always thought it let people underestimate her. But it could be a secret weapon too, he sees now. She's incredible – all the more so, when it felt like it came out of nowhere.

Sam's thoughts must have tempted the universe, somehow. He sits down, leafing through some of the material he can reach. And his eyes just happen to fall on a clipping of a paper from the winter of 1997. He doesn't have to check the date. Not when he has in front of him a picture of the two of them on a skating rink. They had been roughly sixteen, here. So young, and so in love. It's all over their faces, plain as day, even in black and white. "Look," he laughs, holding it up to her.

Maggie takes it distractedly, fussing her glasses up the bridge of her nose. He can see the moment she realizes what she's holding. Sam wonders if she's aware of how hard her other hand grips the edge of the table. He can see her knuckles turning white. Her face is inscrutable.

Until, out of nowhere, it scrunches up. Sam is taken aback at the warmth of recognition it elicits in him. He can decipher, even now, what Maggie looks like when she's thinking hard. A theory that is proven right a handful of seconds later when she jumps to her feet, gasping, *"I have an idea! Oh! I have an idea!"*

For a second, Sam is a ghost haunting his own memory. It was the same face Maggie had once made over coming up with the idea for their AP Chemistry project.

Now, it's this.

MAGGIE

Her excitement had been an unexpectedly dominating wave. She hadn't been able to keep it inside. As is only right, Maggie supposes, she's got to suffer the consequences now.

Consequences, she thinks, her gaze sliding to the man in the passenger seat, *is a good word for Sam Walker.* Despite her every argument otherwise, he had insisted on going with her to the outskirts of town. All because, amidst her eagerness, she'd made the call to Jasper Finch in front of him.

"You don't have to like me," Sam had said when she had begun to protest, "but we've been instructed by the powers that be to work together on this. This is a good opportunity to get used to it."

Maybe it was the way it made sense—and maybe it was just that, running on so little sleep, Maggie didn't have the energy to fight him. Especially when she'd adamantly pressed, "Fine, but I'm going to drive, and you can come along," and he had simply agreed.

Now, he says without looking at her, "If you're going to be the driver, it'd be great if you'd keep your eyes on the road and not kill us." *Oh.* Caught and mortified, Maggie feels her entire face flush. Some of her neck, too.

"Shut up," she mutters, not exactly the paragon of maturity she'd set out to be.

To make matters worse, she suspects he's grinning about it. As much as that thought infuriates her, she refuses to look at him again. *That'll show him,* she decides.

Soon after that, she's parking the car at their—no, *her*—destination. She hops out of the car, shutting the door cacophonously behind herself. She doesn't look back as she leads the way to Jasper's door. He was the town pariah, quirky and odd and overly mythologized into being weirder than he really was. Maggie would consider defending his honor more often if she didn't already know he enjoyed the way kids all over town were a little scared of him. To her, he was a friend.

When he opens the door, he greets her like one. With warm pats on her back, he huddles them into his trailer. He shoots furtive looks her companion's way, though—until Maggie has to introduce him. "Sam's helping me; he's the co-chair heading the committee," she says shortly, and then barrels ahead enthusiastically, adding, "We're going to recreate the first ever winter market from twenty-five years ago! And I was just thinking about it—and of course no pressure at all, I'll never even bring it up again if you say no, Jasper—but you were the first person I thought of when it came to building the rink and some of the décor from the old photos. So, what do you say?"

She knows she's practically pouting at him. It may be slightly manipulative. Jasper, to his credit, looks torn between amusement and fondness. Happily, Maggie accepts it. And then, Jasper suggests, "Tell you *what,* missy," his voice rasps, "how 'bout I do you one better? I'll even make you some winter contraptions for that fancy exhibit you've got to put on."

Maggie doesn't plan on it. Something just whips her around to look at Sam, a look on her face asking, *Are you hearing this?!* Her stomach flips, and then flips again, over the unambiguously impressed look on Sam's face. *So cool,* he mouths to her, smiling broadly around the words. *Wow.* He mimes clapping for her.

He looks so boyish this way, lit up and soft, bright-eyed and kind.

It yanks her sharply back in time. To their past. To that last time she'd seen him before he'd left her—that final break. She can still hear it now, the way he'd shouted at her. How he had told her she only wanted a small life. That she had never been passionate about anything, so she couldn't understand what he was looking for. The way he had taunted her, telling her being safe wasn't everything. He had given her every reason he wasn't going to stay before he had left her for good... in pursuit of everything Maggie wasn't for him.

She has to look away from him now. *It doesn't matter*, she tells herself. Even as her heart rate rises and her head buzzes. *It was a long time ago,* she reminds herself sternly.

What's she supposed to do, when it hurts like it had been only yesterday?

Chapter Four

MAGGIE

IT HADN'T BEEN an easy feat. But they had managed. They'd put their heads together and come up with an elaborate plan that covered both granular and overarching details. Maggie had managed to stuff her feelings down like a long thread of colorful handkerchiefs shoved back up a magician's sleeve, and partaken in a real, true collaboration with a man who had once tap-danced on her heart.

Yet what should have been a reward from the universe for her maturity is instead another opportunity for senseless bedlam. "Are you *kidding* me?" is all she can seem to say, blinking at the phone she's just hung up.

"Maggie," Sam says her name too calmly.

"It's *January,*" she shrieks exasperatedly, just as she'd done to the insipid man who had frantically yelled at her down the line. "Surely it isn't totally absurd to plan for *snow* in *January?* I mean, surely it can't be such a rare, *surprising* symptom of winter, snowfall?" She laughs, but it isn't much of a laugh. Maybe, more accurately, it's better described as vaguely hysterical, somewhat high-pitched wheezing. "I can't. Are you *kidding* me?"

"Maggie!" Now he's exclaiming. *Excellent,* she thinks. One shouldn't panic alone. No. No, no, when one thoroughly messes up the centerpiece of an event they've been tasked to head the committee of, one's co-chair should be panicking with them. She can't spare a look at him to ensure he is.

Her limbs fight stillness, pacing. Anxiety gnaws at her guts like a rat chewing through wires. "I'm gonna lose this place," she says, walking back and forth and back and forth, "I'm totally going to lose this place. Maybe the mayor will just *take it.* Maybe—Oh, maybe he'll turn it into something awful. Out of—Out of *spite.* Politicians can be very spiteful, you know. Even ones who seem perfectly jolly, hunky-dory! So, I'm going to lose the library, and he'll— Maybe I'll just work at Loretta's, and then I can be right there, *right there* when those vicious old twins want to take a swing at me. They can have an easier time telling me all the ways I'm a pathetic, lonely spinster with no prospects in any category of life, and—and I'll just—"

Maggie stops ranting. In fact, Maggie stops *breathing.* Because in that moment, Sam is touching her. Sam Walker has his hands on her —unhesitating, planted on her shoulder, commandeering stillness into her bones—for the first time in two decades. She thinks her mouth opens. She can't tell, though. No words come out.

"I have snow tires," he says simply. Maggie gapes at him, baffled. "So what if those people messed up the delivery? We'll make a list of the props and decorations we need. We will go over to Bridgefield. It's three hours away. I know exactly where they've got an antique shop we can source materials from. It was in the book you saw me reading, that first day we ran into each other."

"Sam, I—" Where that sentence is leading, she doesn't know. She doesn't have to, apparently.

Sam's already saying, "I know you hate me, okay? I know. And I get it. I understand, Maggie. But I still know how to help you. I—I *need* to help you. I would tell you how sorry I am for it all if I thought it would mean a darn thing this many years later, Maggie. But this? I can do this for you. Can you just let me? Please?"

It isn't fair. It isn't fair at all, that he can look at her like this. With that earnest shine to his dark navy eyes, all tender and sincere, piercing, like he can see all the way down to her soul. He shouldn't be able to. After all this time, he shouldn't be able to have such a hold on her. He has no right to get under her skin.

But they both already know there's only one answer to give here.

"Okay," she breathes—and doesn't look at him anymore.

SAM

The drive is strained with agonizing silence. Thoroughly, terribly uncomfortable. Sam hadn't expected anything otherwise.

All surprises today are intent on being an act of God. For all that Maggie had frenziedly ranted on about symptoms of wintertime, he should have thought this through. At least pulled up the forecast on his phone, just to brace himself.

It doesn't feel like much of a mercy for him to be the one behind the wheel this time, though he is grateful for that. But he isn't grateful for much else when, about halfway into the journey, the weather worsens. What had been slight, almost scenic snowfall builds to a storm. Visibility grows more and more obscured until the air can be better described as an arctic fog. Sam's hands clutch at the steering wheel for dear life.

He can hear the guilt permeating Maggie's words when she asks, almost pleading, "What can I do, Sam?"

"Can you just—?" He pauses. On such a risky drive, anxiety prickling down to his very fingertips, it doesn't feel like a real risk to look at her. Especially not when her eyes look stricken, wearing her fear on her face, more vulnerable in front of him than she's been in years. Back before he lost the privilege of witnessing it. Quietly, Sam finishes, "Just distract me?"

It's a good thing his eyes make it back to the road. He only just misses ramming straight into a car, half-wrecked on the side of the highway. Sam gulps audibly.

Maggie has gone so quiet that he's certain she's changed her mind. Then she says, "I don't hate you." She says the words so softly, he almost thinks he's misheard her. In that fragmented moment, Sam discovers he wants it, those words from her. It would make sense, that he's imagining it now. Right? Maggie repeats, "Sam? I don't. I don't hate you."

"What," he blurts. Baffled, strangled.

It has been such a long time since he has heard a real, true laugh from her lips. It's been even longer, Sam knows, since he has been the cause. He can't begrudge being the butt of whatever joke he's become. That sound, he thinks, sounds like coming home.

Maggie quips, "Well, we might die out here. It felt like the right moment to clear things up. So. I don't... Um. Hate you."

Like he's seen happen to her before—he's even laughed at her for it—it's his mouth that opens, then closes. Sam, who doesn't know how to process. Maggie only nods in return, like this unoriginal display of his undiluted shock is just permission to go on.

"I loved you," she says. "Not just—I mean, yes, you were my boyfriend, and yes, it was a bad breakup. You said mean things to me, things that still haunt me on bad days. But you were... also my best friend. My favorite person. And it's one thing to think crushing, cruel, insecure things in your own head. Everybody does that, I think. I think I know that now. It was another for the person I thought saw me, who *really* saw me... to say it all out loud." Maggie pauses. Sam can tell it isn't for his reply, though.

She sounds like she needs the shaky breath she sucks in to carry on. Sam thinks he might just need way, way more than one breath. She's ready before he is, and the irony of that isn't lost on him. He tries to keep his eyes on the road.

"When I saw you the other day, I'd just been handed a very rude reminder of what you'd said. And you weren't wrong, honestly. My life *is* small. It's—It's uneventful. For the most part, I'm okay with that. I even like it. I'm... You found the person *you* needed in that swanky, business titan wife of yours. She's blonde and fancy and stunning. Yes, I've stalked you on social media before. And I was just heartbroken, for longer than I care to admit, that what you needed wasn't me. Because—well, you were that for me."

An icy death wouldn't be the worst thing, Sam considers, when he hears Maggie's voice break. It would have been a better, more substantial admission than what his mouth does offer her. Which is, "I'm divorced."

"Oh," Maggie says. A fair response. "I thought you were in town because of your..."

Sam is quick to say, "I am! Yeah, my dad. I am. But—it was also time, anyway. So, don't take appearances and social media or the baloney I spewed once upon a time like it's fact. One's a stupid highlight reel, and the other was just a loud-mouthed *kid* blowing off steam on someone who didn't deserve it all." He can hear it, that intake of breath that precedes Maggie's arguing. He doesn't regret cutting her off to emphasize, "You *didn't*, Maggie. Just look at what you're doing for the library. That's anything but small. You don't lack passion, Maggie. You never did."

She doesn't say anything. For so long, it stretches to concerning territory. Eventually, Sam has to risk a glance over at her face. Just to find her looking back, her eyes glassy. Her voice is so, so soft when she finally murmurs, "Thank you."

Chapter Five

SAM

SAM LEFT town with one Maggie Foster. It seems he's come back with another. There's no other way to describe how it feels to be handed one of her smiles like it costs her nothing to bestow one on him.

Miraculously, it hasn't stopped there. This Maggie doesn't only grudgingly allow him to help. Just the other day, she actually requested he pick her up. When he drove up to her house, she may not have asked him inside, but she brought him tea. She had remembered the way he'd liked it, and taken a chance. She didn't flinch when their hands brushed over the cup. She didn't run from inviting him to build paper lanterns with her.

All week, they see each other. Every single day, as a matter of fact. And it isn't only seeing, or working on pulling the exhibition together, putting to use the materials and decorations they'd scavenged together in Bridgefield once they had survived the drive there. No, they talk, too. Incessantly. Without running out of things to talk about.

Sam had almost forgotten how thoughtful Maggie was. She asks after his parents and gushes over his niece and nephew. She asks him thoughtful questions about his work as an architect and listens when he answers—not just to be polite, but rather, *really* listens.

Maybe it was what she had confessed in the car. Everything that she had so valiantly put down. It had lightened her, emptied space Sam wasn't sure he deserved. But he couldn't deny that he felt like he'd gotten his very old friend back.

That is if one often wanted to reel close and kiss the living daylights out of one's *friend*. An incurable affliction Sam seems to have come down with.

One that isn't remotely helped by darkness Maggie has cajoled him into walking through tonight. There is no chance she has nefarious intentions. She's been clear: with everything set up for the festival that's in three days, it's time to do a run-through. She is out to prove herself. To prove something about both of them, now that she's accepted they are a team. She can't, and won't, risk not fine-tuning away any last-minute hiccups.

It's endearing. *Too* endearing.

"You ready?" she asks him now. Her voice is hushed but giddy as she feigns lighting up a lantern, then really turns on her phone's flashlight. Her grin is all the brighter for the soft illumination at her own behest.

"Ready," Sam confirms, though he doesn't feel it. He feels winded.

With the rest of Maplewood Grove asleep, they may as well be the only two people in the world. Her body, the only body, the warmest one. He can feel heat radiating from it, seeping in through his layers and burrowing in the spaces between his old, weary bones. Not with a gun to his head could Sam say which one of them leans in enough to cause their fingers to brush. But his heart nearly stops in his chest when Maggie slips her hand into his.

Shock prompts his pivot. It's only a slight turn. Sam hadn't thought they were so close. All he does is bend his head the faintest fraction—and he can count the freckles splattered across her pert little nose. He can taste the chocolatey sweetness on her breath, and knows it's from the chocolate bar he'd slipped into her coat pocket earlier that day.

Maggie's mouth begins to shape something. No sound escapes her. Sam feels his lips part, and knows he didn't plan it...

"*Golly!*" Someone hollers from the side. Maggie recoils instantly, startling so hard she drops her phone with a yelp and a clatter. Like a snap of fingers has jolted her out of a trance, she blinks dazedly. Sam pleads with his mouth to say something, say *anything* when the look on her face has become too familiar to him. He can already tell what's coming.

His mouth fails him. Maggie's feet don't fail her. "*Loretta!*" she exclaims and rushes off. Already she's chattering, exclaiming about the experience they've been brewing together for days. It doesn't matter how quickly Maggie flees; he can't unhear the alarm in her voice, coating every word she expels under the guise of excitement.

MAGGIE

Over the years, her feet must have charted this path hundreds of times. Having lived all her life in this small town, coincidence has brought her to the same pavement her boots traverse now. That makes all the more stark that it's for the first time in many, many years, the afternoon finds Maggie Foster returning to the Walkers' residence on purpose. With every step toward the front door, the familiar chime of the doorbell echoed in her memory.

Mrs. Walker is almost immediately opening the door. Maggie would have been a fool not to expect a surprised reaction. From everything she'd learned from Sam about his life and relationships, she had deduced he wasn't keeping his parents apprised of their murky relationship status. (In a world the tightrope dance spurred by a mixture of denial and desire could actually be called a 'relationship.') She just hadn't anticipated that surprise to manifest with such... *delight*.

Yet that's what she's greeted with. Warmth, and a face that lights up at the sight of her, and arms that reel her into a tight embrace she really *means*. "Maggie Foster," Mrs. Walker sighs, squeezing her. "Now aren't you a sight for sore eyes, honey pie."

"Who is it, Elise?" Mr. Walker asks from the living room.

"It's *Maggie!*" his wife exclaims, excitedly, so genuinely thrilled by Maggie's impromptu appearance.

On her walk over, Maggie had talked up a big game to herself. She had assured herself of all kinds of things: how she wasn't one to chicken out, that she wanted to be bolder, the way one of the biggest regrets in her life has been not speaking up enough and letting her embittered resentments devour her faith and self-respect. She had told herself, stubbornly, that she may not have a clue what was going on between her and Sam, but she knew she didn't plan to be afraid to face it. She *wouldn't* be.

That had been before this, though. Now, one hug later, her adolescence comes racing back in a wave that pulls her under. So much—even most—of her youth had been spent under this roof. The way she's welcomed, it's like she never even left.

Maggie's head doesn't know what to think. Her heart doesn't know how to hold this much tenderness at once. She's so overwhelmed, she almost forgets who she's come for.

Almost. But not really.

Maggie hears Sam's footsteps patter down the stairs, and it transports her to twenty-some years ago. She recognizes that gait. That terrifies her a little. She had been so sure she'd gotten him out from under her skin, but it only took a few careless words for all the old feelings to come rushing back—fear, hope, longing, and resentment all tangled up together. Maggie had spent years convincing herself that Sam's departure hadn't destroyed her, that she had built a life just fine without him. But deep down, she knew better. The truth was, every failed relationship, every moment of doubt, could be traced back to that day when Sam had left, proving to her that love wasn't something she could count on. And now, here he was again, stirring up feelings she wasn't ready to confront. Frozen in his living room doorway, Maggie has never felt more obvious in her life.

To his credit, when Sam catches sight of her, he greets with a "hi," and the look on his face is torn between fond bafflement and unnerved awe. Still, he doesn't shy away from inviting, "Will you come sit down with me? We can talk over the festival."

Much the same way it had been a regular occurrence once upon a time, sitting turns to tea. Tea is filled with uproarious laughter and inside jokes she's in on. An invitation to stay for lunch isn't a suggestion, it's an insistence bordering on a demand. After all this time, it's everything. It's fast, and it's overwhelming—and, at the same time, it's a fatal bout of homesickness letting up. Her stomach should be in excellent shape with the acrobatic flips it attempts over and over.

When lunchtime comes, it brings Sam's older brother, Solomon Walker, all dapper in his uniform and handsome with that broad, winning smile of his. He calls the visit a "drop by check-in," which annoys Sam for some reason he isn't keen to discuss.

Maggie doesn't prod. Not now, any more than she had back then. There was friction between the two Walker boys and always had been. Anyone could see there was love and respect there, right alongside brotherly competition the two had never grown out of. She had no intention of interfering. When the two of them decide to go out to the patio, Maggie stays with Mrs. Walker, devotedly helping mash potatoes, despite Sol's transparent attempts at persuading her outside with them.

It's Mr. Walker she can't say no to—and wouldn't have been able to, patient suffering from a recent stroke or not—once he asks her to call his boys inside. He can feel them getting rowdy outside, he says.

Just outside the window, she can see the beer bottle Sam's lithe fingers are wrapped around the neck of. She can hear him snap, "Some of us aren't perpetually stuck in high school. I don't even fit in this town anymore—and Maggie Foster *is* Maplewood Grove." She could swear she hears her heart break right there. Yet, she can't move.

For that moment, Maggie isn't angry. Maybe, she considers, she isn't anything. Maybe, she changes her mind a millisecond later, I'm angry with *myself*. She deserves to be. *How did I let him back under my skin?* she has to ask herself. There's no answer she can stomach.

In a haze, she says goodbye to his family. It's all she can handle before she has to rush out, right past him, without looking back. She doesn't want to give him the satisfaction.

He doesn't understand. No, he grasps at her elbow, alarm all over his face. Maggie screams, she just screams at him, maybe just a little bit for the slip of a girl whose heart he'd once broken before: "Who the *hell* do you think that you are? Oh, I heard you. I—Who do you think you are, to judge me? To still be judging me. You don't even know who I am. You think—what, that all my life has been is waiting for you? I am a grown woman. I have a home that I *own*. I have a group of smart, like-minded women to talk to, with whom I discuss quality literature every week. Unlike you, I know how to correctly use 'with whom.' My parents adore me. I may not be some hoity-toity, glitzy city girl with bold ambitions and *unnecessarily long legs,* but I am a good person. A *loyal* person. The kind who is solid, reliable, and stays. So, you were right, back then – I do have a small life. And I am proud of it. Why don't you get out of my town, away from me, and we'll pretend the last two weeks were nothing but a fever dream?" Sam tries to talk, and Maggie revels in how her voice cuts. "*Don't.* I don't have anything to say to you. And you have nothing I want to hear."

Chapter Six

MAGGIE

MAGGIE DOESN'T UNDERSTAND how she's gotten here again. But she knows she can't dwell. There's no time. She doesn't have the capacity. Even with all the fixings ready for the festival, paper lanterns, quaint candles in gorgeous candle holders, and Dot prepared with her wisdom to impart, Maggie still can't let up.

The simple, painful truth of it is that Maggie knows, that once she started crying over Sam Walker, she just may never stop. Hasn't she wasted enough time doing that already? She could punish herself. Torture herself. But it wouldn't help. With every passing minute, Maggie doubts anything could.

An event as expansive as the Winter Heritage Festival requires no end of attention. Apart from the decor, there are plenty of details to keep an eye on. Whether it's about food vendors or organizing people into manageable files of lines, Maggie keeps on top of it. It's almost good to have it, to pour herself into like an abyss.

But it would have been a lie to pretend there wasn't a part of her that thought: I'll show the Carlton twins I *don't* need a man. Definitely not a man who is Sam Walker.

When she turns around though, Maggie doesn't know why she's even surprised. All it takes is thinking his name for him to show up these days. Her fondness for it has evaporated as swiftly as it had returned. There had been so many years when she had wanted him here. Waited for him. She had dreamt of the things she would say to him if she ever saw him again. So many things ranging from graceful yet withering remarks to moments of magnanimous forgiveness. Today she just feels cold. She thinks about how the universe has a sick sense of humor. Though it would make sense if he was actually a demon. Lord knew he definitely had enough traits in common with one.

She finds it effortless to ignore him. She turns around and tells herself he isn't there. She has more practice with him being absent than she does with him being in her space by now. What did a few weeks of him being here, apologetic and sweet, have on the years and years she'd spent feeling like a fool over him? Being abjectly heartbroken. Crying and praying, then hating and damning him, on and on in cyclical patterns that made no sense and only ever hurt.

Still, it chafes at her that Sam doesn't react to it. Maggie feels him behind her; a warm, solid wall she can't risk leaning against. He's made it perfectly clear that he will always let her fall. It drives her crazy that he just starts talking and carries on like he knows she's listening.

He doesn't need her to say anything back when he tells her: "When I was in the city, I... I wasn't good at sleeping. Even when I did, I didn't often wake up feeling rested. And I got used to it. To just feeling a little fried. To walking through my life with—with this hollowness in my chest. Something I didn't want to pay attention to. Something I kept myself too busy to think about too hard. Until I was back here. And I saw you, and I made you laugh again, and you looked at me like you used to... And it started to fill that hollowness

up with warmth. Warmth and light and goodness; simple, uncomplicated goodness. I wasn't– When I said that to Sol, I didn't mean that
as some messed up criticism, Maggie. I meant that I have gotten so far
away from who I set out to be. You aren't– You aren't *small*. You're
like a favorite spot on a favorite couch that someone looks forward to
after a long, unbearable day. That I look forward to. It doesn't have
to be grand to be what I need. I meant that I miss you. I miss you,
and I know it's my own fault that I do. But I've been homesick for
longer than I've wanted to admit it—and you're home. You're home
to me. Whatever else you want to hate me for, okay. I get it. But don't
hate me for this. If by tonight you've really decided you can't stand to
share this town with me, I'll go. I won't put you through that."

Maggie can't move. Her limbs have forgotten how. By the time
she makes herself turn around, Sam is already gone.

SAM

His personal universe may feel totally eclipsed, but lanterns dot the sky all over Maplewood Grove that night. Sam isn't surprised. He had known from the moment Maggie had come up with the idea that she was going to execute something extraordinary. The luminary walk transformed the snowy streets of Maplewood Grove into something magical. Lanterns crafted by the town's artisans lined the paths, casting a warm glow on the frosty ground. Dot Simmons, the town historian, led the procession, her voice clear as she recounted the stories of the luminaries—residents who had shaped Maplewood Grove's past. As they passed the old courthouse, Dot spoke of its founding, weaving in tales of love, loss, and perseverance. The crowd walked in reverent silence, each step a reminder of the town's resilience through the generations. Sam found himself drawn to the history, feeling a deep connection to the town he had once fled.

Despite his somber malaise, he trails after the crowd Dot Simmons leads through the makeshift passage of the Luminary Walk. The same snow that felt so sinister only days ago on a highway was now nothing less than enchanting. It was fascinating how perspective could shape an experience for a single person. Sam listens to Dot regale the crowd with the town's history the same way parents tell their children fairy tales or bedtime stories.

Halfway through the passage, his attention begins to drift. He can't help but think of a few nights ago, this same path led by a different woman; one who'd laced her fingers through his and almost kissed him. He's so lost in his yearning, Sam seriously considers whether he's losing his mind when Maggie cuts through the crowd and walks right up to him.

Her voice is hushed as she asks, "Can we talk please?" Sam feels his head nod shakily, involuntarily. "Do you wanna go first?"

"Yeah. I—Yes. I shouldn't have eavesdropped. That's very rude." She looks like a startled deer.

His heart sinks. "Oh. That's fine."

Maggie looks at him like she doesn't know what else to say to that. He wonders if this is where she runs again. Already, his hands itch to stop her from doing just that. How unnecessary. "I don't know how to trust you," she blurts. "I–I heard you. I hear you. And I believe you; I believe that this is how you feel. But you feel it now. You feel it now, and you felt it once, and you left me then. You said cruel things to me, and you left me to sit with them for years. And now you're here. And it just feels like you're doing it to me all over again."

Maggie felt the familiar ache return, the one she had learned to push deep down over the years. Sam had been the center of her world once, and when he left, it wasn't just her heart that shattered—it was her confidence in love, in herself. She had spent years piecing herself back together, vowing never to let anyone close enough to break her like that again. The anger, the sadness, the betrayal—they had become part of her, and now, standing here in front of him, she wondered if she'd ever truly healed. Could she let go of the past long enough to believe that this time might be different? That Sam had changed? Could she even risk it?

"I'm not trying to do something to you," Sam protests, going from defensive to feeble in record time. "I'm not—I didn't. I didn't feel this before. I'm not—"

He can almost hear Maggie swallow. "Did you love me then?"

"Maggie—" He isn't sure his heart is beating.

"Sam, please. Just. Did you?"

She didn't know. All this time later, and she still had to ask. Whether Maggie did or didn't, Sam isn't sure he can forgive himself for this—for the look of abject trepidation buried in every line and divot of Maggie's beautiful face. "Yeah. I did. But I loved you in a way I didn't know how to take care of. I was a stupid, lost teenager. I'm not, now. I've lived life. It hasn't been a bad one, but it hasn't been free of trials either. Now, when I say that word—love—I know what it means. I know what it encompasses."

"Now—Do you love me now?" Her eyes are glossed with a film of tears she blinks over.

"I don't know that I ever stopped," Sam confesses hoarsely. "It doesn't feel like I did. But I don't know you anymore. I just—I want to know you again. It broke my heart to see yours break. And it's taken me years to realize that I never stopped loving you. I kept trying to convince myself that leaving was the right thing, that I needed something different, but nothing has ever compared to what I had with you. I'm terrified, Maggie. Terrified that I'll hurt you again, that I'll mess this up because I couldn't love you right the first time. But I'm not that foolish kid anymore. I'm here now, and I want to do this right. I need to learn how to love you right this time. I don't want this to be another mistake. I don't want us to go through that again."

Maggie's voice is a whisper. But she's so close, he doesn't miss it. He couldn't. He doesn't want to miss anything about her ever again. Even when she says, "I don't know how to let you."

"Do you want to?"

"...Yes."

Adamantly, Sam nods. "Then let's start there," he says.

Maggie feels her breath catch in her throat. The years of hurt, the walls she had carefully built, all feel like they are crumbling at his words. She had spent so long guarding herself, convincing her heart that she was fine without him, that she didn't need anyone. Yet, standing here in front of Sam, with his raw honesty and the sincerity in his eyes, she realizes something that shakes her to her core—she wants this. She wants to trust him again, to believe that this time would be different. But it isn't easy to let go of the past. It isn't easy to forget the pain he had caused her. And yet, for the first time in years, she feels hope. Not blind, naive hope, but the cautious hope of someone who had been broken before but is willing to take the risk because the reward might just be worth it. Maggie straightens her shoulders, her resolve solidifying. This isn't about forgiving him for the past. This is about choosing her own happiness, on her own terms.

"I didn't just come back to Maplewood Grove for my parents. Something tugged me, kept me here—and I know it's you. It doesn't feel empty now. This, right here..." Sam draws closer, taking Maggie in his arms. She trembles but doesn't pull away from him. "It feels whole, with you. Can we take it one step at a time?"

Maggie whispers, "What's step two?" She's already reeling him in.

Sam's lips meet hers, molding against her warm, giving mouth. She tastes so sweet, like a dream. She tastes like coming home. Sam lets himself, gladly.

As their lips meet, Maggie realizes that this wasn't the end of her story, but the beginning of a new chapter. One she is writing for herself. She isn't the same woman Sam left behind all those years ago, and this time, it's going to be different. Not because of him, but because of her. She is stronger now, and she will make sure that whatever comes next, she will face it head-on—with or without him.

Chapter Seven

THE CO-CHAIRS of the carnival committee bask in the raucous applause the entire town showers them with at the end of the night. Neither the handsome, proud architect nor the rosy-cheeked and bespectacled librarian mind how publicly their triumph is celebrated. One might just say the pair is too lost, gazing lovingly into one another's eyes, to take much notice.

Their celebration, no matter in the dead center of the town festivities, feels private. Together, guiding each other onto an ice rink, they hold each other as steady as a mother goat to her kid as it learns how to steady its shaky legs and walk on its own. Maggie Foster and Sam Walker do one better: they untether years worth of baggage from their shoulders for a moment in time they gift to each other, and sway onto the ice together. The blades of their skates lash at and etch whimsical curlicues into the surface.

When esteemed local journalist, Diana Hayes, is seen floating through the hullabaloo snapping evocative photographs of the spectacular festival for a feature, she captures the two in an embrace not unlike one memorialized in a newspaper from 1997: a dark-haired woman with her eyes latched to the grinning face of a handsome man, her lips pressed to the apple of his cheek. If possible, this iteration of the couple, decades later, emanates a different, softer kind of devotion.

Maybe Diana Hayes even catches the man suggesting ways to spruce up the library with a couple of extra architectural additions he could suggest to the mayor. It may not be front-page news, but it is significant when Maggie Foster assures him, "I think you'll find your place in Maplewood Grove again just fine, Sam."

The End.

Sweet Storm

A SMALL TOWN FORCED PROXIMITY
ROMANCE

Chapter One

DIANA

Some people mistake routine for predictability. Diana Hayes can sympathize. Then she looks around the room. More importantly, she looks at the three other women left around the circle they've been sitting in for the past half hour. They linger long after the other members of their increasingly popular book club have vacated the premises. The same way that they do every Thursday evening. Then, Diana doesn't see anything predictable about it.

She doesn't understand how anyone possibly could.

Occupational hazard, she supposes. It's more than that, though. Her appreciation for human beings, in all their intricacies and contradictions, precedes her ability to speak coherent sentences. Diana can't remember ever not feeling that way. Frankly, she can't be blamed, she thinks.

She feels affirmed just watching her friend, Maggie Foster. The way Maggie ducks her head, color flooding her cheeks and a helpless, lovesick grin on her lips, even as she tells Rachel and Izzie to knock it off. Neither Rachel nor Izzie does, obviously.

"It's okay to admit you're in love, Mags." Rachel nudges Maggie.

Maggie gasps in mock affront that isn't as believable as Maggie seems to think it is.

Izzie can't help snickering. "Definitely ready to have his babies. Abandoning the Spinster Resistance—" a name Isabel Martinez (Izzie, to the inner circle) has suggested for the book club before, and now uses to refer to the four of them, "—for shame, woman. Sending back feminism, one nauseatingly cute date at a time."

The teasing, Rachel's gentler and Izzie's more unabashed, is as good-natured as it is deserved. After all, only a little more than a month ago, Maggie had been swearing up and down that the handsome architect Sam Walker who had come to town was a part of her past she felt nothing but disdain for.

Now, just a mention of his name prompts a blush. Lately, Maggie has been *giggling*.

For people who have known her much longer than a month, it's jarring. Delightful, too. Mostly, it's just proof that people change. Even when they returned to the same places and things; sometimes, even when they returned to the same people. That's the beauty of the human experience. She's always considered it to be a point of pride that cataloging it is what she gets to do for a living.

All three continue to quip back and forth. Diana watches, unbearably fond of these women who fill her life with such dynamic color. Her lack of participation could go amiss. She isn't the only one just spectating. Patty Sullivan, not a member of their little club, but owner of the fabulous, whimsical location that hosts it and a dear pal to Diana herself, laughs breezily in the background too.

Except, it's rarer for Patty to butt in.

One of the few downsides of being the resident journalist in the room is that, when you go an entire evening without asking a single question, it doesn't go unnoticed. So, despite her every hope otherwise, it still doesn't exactly surprise Diana when Izzie's shrewd gaze zeroes in on her. Lamely, she blows Izzie a kiss. Izzie snorts, then undercuts the caustic gesture when she mimes catching it. The way she always does. But the look on Izzie's face is knowing.

"Yes?" Diana asks airily, feigning ignorance regardless.

"Di."

"That's an awful thing to tell your friend to do, Isabel," Diana tuts. "And *definitely* too harsh a reaction for a little quiet." Izzie bursts into laughter at that. It's predictable, but it isn't routine. How could a laugh be that? You can love someone for years and have it never get old if you love them well enough. Somehow, the reminder that blooms in her is what prompts her to admit, "I'm okay. I'm just a little in my head."

It's Rachel who asks, "About what, hon?" She isn't the oldest of them, but sometimes she feels it to Diana, who is the youngest. Then again, being a single mom ages you. Diana's been watching Rachel do it for months; the newest of their ragtag little group. She doesn't think she could do what Rachel does.

But her experience has embedded a certain maternal warmth in the very fabric of her person. The way she asks, Diana is helpless to answer, "I've just been feeling burnt out. Not very inspired, which is new, deeply uncomfortable territory for me." But it isn't in her nature to dwell despondently. *What will it solve?* She's asked herself more than once over the past few weeks. Today, a better question is on her mind, like Scrabble tiles rearranged for better points: *What will solve it?*

Diana explains, "I've been feeling like my well is running dry, creatively. It's been eating at me for weeks. But..." Her voice steadies with newfound resolve. "I think I've found something that might change everything."

Maggie's curiosity is piqued. "Oh? What kind of something?"

Diana offers a small, almost secretive smile, choosing her words carefully. "Let's just say... sometimes a spark of curiosity can light a fire. But for now, it's still an ember." Izzie, bless her, senses Diana's malaise. It would be imperceptible to most eyes, but not to a pair that knows her. She's grateful for it, the privilege of being known—she lets it shine through her laughter when Izzie teases, "You realize how unfortunately hilarious your last name makes this farm-centric metaphor, don't you, Hayes?"

"I didn't say I'd lost all supply of wit, did I?"

The chains around her snow tires clang noisily as she drives through the town in record time. It may not be the ideal weather to be driving in, but Diana is rarely, if ever, dissuaded by nerves. Fortunately—or not, depending on one's perception of the matter—there is plenty at work to fry her nerves.

"What's one more item on the list?" she asks herself. "Company, that's what."

Her reflection in the windshield looks contemplative at best. It's a sight she's familiar with. In a certain light, Diana can reframe anything. Another occupational hazard. "This could be a full-circle situation," she reminds herself. "Came to this town for a fluff piece, decided to stay forever. Can't feel a pulse in a single thing going on, so now I'm heading to the edge of town, chasing a prospective story with *meat*. The article's already writing itself, isn't it? It is. Of course it is." There's no one else in the car to point out she doesn't have much of a future as a lawyer. But that's fine. Diana already knows. She finds she can, at least, still humor herself.

It isn't a small feat when she's going out on a limb, likely on the precipice of a felony, just to feel the thrill she's lost in this small town she loves so dearly. "You have to suffer for your art," she quips to her tense features in the rearview mirror. The irony isn't lost on her that it's an *artist*, a far more literal one than Diana herself can claim to be, that she's in the pursuit of currently.

Though, in all fairness, that hadn't been the plan. Diana had first spotted Logan Black weeks ago, a figure shrouded in mystery as he rode into town. There was something about the way he carried himself—like a man burdened with more than his share of secrets. At first, she had brushed it off as a fleeting curiosity. But the more she uncovered about his past—the sudden retreat from fame, the cryptic articles that trailed off into speculation—the more she realized this was the story that could pull her out of the creative desert she had been wandering.

Amidst a series of blurry photos she'd snuck, there had been one clear enough to plug into Google's image-search function. It was unveiled otherwise. Fortunately, the man was far from a nobody. Her search, even wrong, wasn't without fruitful results. He wasn't just an artist. He's an infamous recluse. Well-documented—or he had begun to grow to be, two years ago, before he had dropped off the face of the earth at the *peak* of his career. Just after his breakout exhibition had received rave reviews across the board.

The only available number for him was that of his listed representative. Who, when Diana had finally been able to get her on the phone, had sassed, "Listen, doll, if *you* can reach him, have him get back to *me*, huh?" before the line had gone dead.

She'd mostly been left to the mercy of the internet. Nevertheless, Diana hadn't had to dive too deeply into the search results to unearth some solid facts. There had been enough information to know, though more than one interviewer had described Mr. Black as reserved, taciturn, and generally disinclined towards sharing about his origins or inspirations— he wasn't from Maplewood Grove.

The second time she'd caught sight of him, he'd been meandering outside of the grocery store. He seemed cold, only offering clipped, unfeeling responses to the cashier when he'd tried to make conversation.

"Maybe that's not enough of a reason to stalk the man, but..." *Maybe 'stalk' is putting it too harshly,* she considers from the other side, before she has to shake that thought away. That was precisely what it had been when she'd followed him to the same location she's heading to now, having hit the end of her own self-prescribed time-line. It wasn't like she hadn't sent him letter after letter for two weeks straight. The man seemed determined to stay unreachable. Diana is just determined, period.

Not naive, though. It's a selfish pursuit, and she knows it. She hadn't expected a cozy welcome from the man. But... she also hadn't experienced this deep-seated tug at her guts in so, so long. Nor the electric anticipation that lingers like a film of static over her skin. All she's been able to think is: *I know where he is. I have to know his story. I have to.*

She isn't ready to let go of that hunger yet. She hasn't had it in years. It had been an accidental discovery—an unintended friction against a sixth sense that had been lulled into complacency—but it felt like a sign from the universe. *Maybe,* her conscience supplies, *that's a self-indulgent excuse.* "Maybe," Diana agrees. "Too late now." The mansion is already in sight.

She looks out of her window at the sky, dark with plumes of clouds lurking like an augury. She sends out a little prayer to the universe, asking it to hold out, in more than one way. She needs this —and, out of all the things Diana Hayes has learned how to do in this life, blinking first just isn't one of them.

LOGAN

The eeriness of this place is seeping into him, Logan thinks. Like mold, poisoning him. He isn't unaware of how dramatic that thought is. It isn't even a seriously original one. But one has to take creativity where it flows, don't they? Especially in the middle of a drought.

So much of creation is bundled up in a unique perspective. In the past, he's heard it likened to a plant, and inspiration posed as the sunlight it needs to thrive. *Even cacti need it,* the woman had added pointedly, scowling his way. He'd found amusement in it then. Now, all he feels is withered.

Logan had come here—seeking solace, maybe even redemption. In this abandoned mansion, he had hoped to rebuild something, but instead, it only reflected the decayed state of his own soul. The walls seemed to whisper forgotten memories, much like the ones he tried to suppress—memories of Gus Laurier, his mentor, who had once told him, "True art is born from suffering, but it's not meant to break you." The words haunted him now because they rang hollow in his heart.

Here, cobwebs aren't just littering the bone dome of his skull. Haunted. Instead of grandeur, there is decay. *There is a metaphor here,* he thinks. A thought that never gets the chance to finish itself. He never was good with words. That was why he'd leaned into this in the first place, wasn't it? To speak and be understood, in a way words had never allowed. An artist.

Not for the first time that week, Logan wonders if he can even still call himself that.

He could ask himself the question out loud. Wail it like a distressed ghoul, just to have it echo through this vast, empty mausoleum. But he is too tired. No one ever told him how exhausting it could be, to do nothing at all.

To have no one to speak to.

Then again, it isn't as if he enjoys the alternative. It had taken Logan approximately twenty minutes in the small town of Maple-wood Grove to discover that every single resident was concerningly cheerful and painfully chatty. Painful, of course, to him.

He doesn't think he can be faulted for fleeing. Right back to the mansion, despite how *freezing* it is. It may have been an involuntary escape... but he stands by it. Especially since showing his face had somehow given someone out there an idea to come bother him. Every day, for days now, someone rang the bell. Every single day. This, Logan had decided, was how Boo Radley must have felt.

Still, he refused to answer the door. Fine, partly, it was because he had no energy to trek through the truly labyrinthian garden to get to the massive, ornate gate to chit-chat with some random, potentially irritating person. How was he even meant to explain his own presence? What on earth would a sane man be doing in a gigantic mansion that appeared, for all intents and purposes, *abandoned?* The conclusion draws itself, he finds.

This place may actually be haunted, besides. Logan finds he isn't opposed to it. *A potential source of inspiration?* It could be.

No sooner does the thought flit through his vacant head that, by some serendipitous force, a cacophonous knock sounds against the door. Not the bell on the gate, but rather –

Did someone else have a key?

"Looking for a sign is a sign," someone important had once told Logan Black.

This is a sign. He creeps through the hallways he's grown accustomed to pacing in the middle of the night, finding his way through this wing of the mansion to the front door. The handle may as well be a handful of ice cubes when he wrenches it open.

Oh, he thinks. *Oh.* No.

It isn't a ghost. It's... A blonde.

Chapter Two

LOGAN

Blonde is a lazy way to describe her. Proof, Logan thinks, of how out of practice he is.

He appraises her conscientiously. Then tries again. She's a petite woman, but tall enough that the fact isn't immediately apparent. Her shade of blonde is natural. Even cast in shadows, it's a sunshine waterfall. *She looks like spring,* Logan muses. Eyes green as a four-leaf clover, paired with an unpainted, rosebud mouth, chapped from the cold. The texture is anything but off-putting. Her skin resembles a puddle of milk, with freckles dusted like a spoonful of instant coffee. Her cheeks are marred with splotches. The small, slightly crooked line of her teeth chatters – despite the regal navy turtleneck and thick coat she wears, dressed sensibly if not fashionably. The coat looks like tweed. This texture, too, makes his fingers itch.

Logan blinks dubiously. He can't ascertain whether her skin is as translucent as it momentarily appears. Maybe she *is* a ghost.

"You're an awfully hard man to reach, Mr. Black," she says. *Oh.* Her voice is exactly as sweet as one would expect from a face like hers.

Interesting, that. Logan has found that it is rare for that to be the case. People typically surprise him in the most unpleasant of ways.

It isn't until he jerks back from his own last name that he realizes how frozen he is. If he'd thought the mansion had been cold... It's practically summertime in here, compared to the arctic chill that pours in through the open door. A hapless, violent shiver wracks through his body. He looks down. That is when he remembers what he is wearing. "This isn't my coat," he blurts out, eyes wide as saucers over the fur monstrosity cloaking him.

The woman holds a hand out, smiling warmly. "Noted," she says. "I'm Diana Hayes. May I come in?" Logan is frozen from more than just the cold. He can't find a word to say to her. Before his mind can crawl its way to a resounding *No,* she's taken it to be a *Yes,* already, and steps right on in.

She shuts the door behind herself. *Diana Hayes.*

Logan gapes at her, speechless over her liberal audacity. This unwelcome intrusion... no matter how lovely a sight she was. The dim light of the expansive foyer illuminates her features softly. But he still remembers—praise the Lord—that he is here for a very singular purpose.

"Please go away," he says succinctly.

The woman must be hard of hearing since she does the very opposite. She takes another two steps, turning in a leisurely circle. Her light eyes apprize the trappings of the room. She wears her amazement, Diana. Logan scowls in defense. Undeterred, she asks, "Is this your property?" Light, airy voice.

Logan remains silent. There is no right answer here. There are only multiple wrong ones. Determinedly, his lips purse to a firm line. He pins her with a blank stare that usually does the trick when it comes to unnerving people a safe distance away from him. Not with Diana Hayes, apparently.

"It's not," she answers herself, too cheerfully. He decides she is at least half as odious as she is stunning. "There are legal records of these things, you know. Technically, this property is still part of Maplewood Grove. You, however, are from New Orleans. Right, Mr. Black?"

His stomach churns painfully. He feels ill. "Who—" he grapples, "—are you?" She would make a good villain in a thriller, he thinks. Beautiful. Creepy. Not unlike the mansion she's shoved her impish little nose into, in fact.

"We've been through this, Mr. Black," she says. Then quickly amends, "Logan? Can I call you Logan? Nevertheless: I'm—"

"Mr. Black is fine," he interrupts coolly. A shameless lack of manners, but he can't be blamed for it. Surely, he can't be blamed. This woman is unhinged.

She laughs, and it is such a deep, full-bodied sound, that Logan is the one unnerved. "Oh, Logan, you're a funny man. Are you sure the fur coat isn't yours?" She has the gall to quip. She teases him like... Like they are age-old friends. They aren't. He has one friend—*had* one friend—and he's gone now. Logan blinks at her. She keeps on talking. "I'm a journalist. And, to be fair, I've been writing to you for close to a fortnight. I had to take matters into my own hands. So, I'm here, out on a limb, to say: I'd love the opportunity to interview you."

All he can do is look at her. And look at her and look at her. She appears, albeit with a vaguely terrifying smile spread across her lips, entirely serious. There's only one thing to do.

He turns on his heel and walks away.

DIANA

Diana had heard of artists being moody. But she had to admit, she'd envisioned 'moody' as passionate. Someone prone to getting heated, sure, but with *conviction.*

Logan Black possesses all the heat of the Abominable Snowman. Yet, when he walks away from her, Diana is left trembling from the temperature that drops in his absence. She's lost feeling in her fingers —or is getting there. Rubbing her palms together helps nothing.

What choice does she have but to follow after him? "That wasn't a no," she chirps, in a manner she can only hope is beguiling. Unfortunately, even without seeing his face, she can tell, just from the set of his shoulders shrouded in fur she *hopes* is of the faux variety, that he's stiffened. Some of her zeal ebbs.

She sighs. Still, she refuses to let it be one of defeat. Her breath fogs in front of her. Curiosity turns her head. The windows along the hall are uncovered. She can see the snow progress from flurries to thicker, quicker-falling clumps of ice. When Diana looks back ahead, he's turning a corner. She chases after him like a shadow. As his steps quicken, so do hers.

She can only hope he knows where he's going. Besides, underneath a certain lens, one might even say he's giving her a tour—and that, she wouldn't mind. There's an aura the very walls exude. Its grandeur is weathered and peeling, but not lost. Cobwebs hang like fairy lights between chandeliers and intricate crown molding that lines the length of the ceilings, growing more pronounced around the pillars that sideline countless windows. The chandelier crystals still twinkle, like frozen stars. The webs cast a net that mutes its light, softening it.

Diana walks right into his chest. She had missed his halting, forget noticing his body pivoting to face hers. Somehow, he's the one who looks winded. "Hi?" she huffs.

"I don't want to do an interview," Logan says, syllables clipped. His breath fogs, too. Condensation coats her cheeks.

"Why?" she asks. "Off the record."

He's gaping at her again. Diana is certain he doesn't know how comical the sight is. Then again, she suspects he wouldn't be keen to give her any rewards for managing not to laugh. He looks anything but amused. "I—Well, I just don't." He chokes out the words.

It isn't as if she hadn't expected that she'd need to wear him down. "You won't do an interview," Diana echoes. "You won't tell me why. Look, I'm going to write. And I've got every right to explore whatever subject matter I find intriguing. Artistic license and all; I'm sure you can appreciate that? Now, maybe that subject matter is you. Maybe it's this mansion."

The color drains from his face. "The mansi— *Why?*"

Diana doesn't understand the high-pitched hysteria in his tone. She doesn't let it deter her, though. "Look around," she insists. "Clearly, there's a story here. Can't you just feel it in the air?"

"That's called mildew and dust." Still unamused. What a *grouch*.

She tries: "You're an artist—"

"Allegedly."

She laughs again, but it's mostly a bark of exasperation if she's being honest. "Aren't you meant to have a more poignant sense of perspective?" she demands.

"Am I?"

"*Are you?*"

His eyes narrow. In suspicion, Diana reads. "What do you know?" he asks.

"I'm not fascinated by the things I don't, Logan," she answers. She doesn't staunch the earnestness that colors the words. It isn't a tactic, but maybe it'll still work.

For a long beat, he says nothing at all. Until... "You must either be a very good reporter, or a very bad one." He doesn't sound put off. Diana doesn't miss that.

"Allegedly," she replies, a smirk playing at her lips.

His expression shifts, pain flashing across it. "Can you just leave? I'm not an artist anymore," he mutters, voice strained.

Diana feels an unexpected pull to dig deeper. It's not just curiosity—it's something she can't quite explain.

"Logan. Do you really think I'd come all this way just to—"
"Harass me?" Logan supplies unhelpfully.

"—make this much of an effort, if I hadn't done the research that warranted?" she finished as if he hadn't interrupted at all, smiling sweetly.

The man looks fazed, that's for sure. "What kind of research?"

"On the record?" Logan looks at her flatly. Diana laughs lightly and shrugs. "Worth a try," she allows, nodding to herself. "Your work. It was very well-received. And then you fell off the face of the art world. The regular world, too. People don't just... do that. You weren't bad at it. Any aspect of it, from the looks of it. There are interviews of you online, presenting your work. You're excellent, Logan. Charismatic, evocative. *Not* without a poignant sense of perspective."

Somehow, her candor has only rendered his features unreadable. "Look," he says, and the word sounds painfully tender when it leaves his full mouth. "The person you're looking for isn't here. I'm sure you're a nice person. But I'm... I'm just not interested. This isn't my property, no, but presuming you've got basic human decency, could you just – go? This... It isn't going to happen. Please, just accept that, and go."

"...Are you okay, Logan?" Diana finds herself whispering. It isn't the question she had planned to ask. She'd had a plan. But there's just something about it. About the utter devastation that lines his features just then. He is only thirty-two. He looks so much older than that.

"No," he answers. His honesty surprises them both, she sees. He doesn't take it back, though. He repeats: "No, I'm not."

Slowly, she nods. Accepts that, cradling it in her hands as carefully as she can. Especially since she has to confess: "Well, I can't go. My—" He looks betrayed. Diana hurries to explain, her head shaking with fervor, "No. No, don't misunderstand. My car is just probably buried by now. I sat outside the gate for a while before I finally jumped it. So, unless you've got a shovel, you're pretty much stuck with me until it melts."

He's back to blinking at her. He whips back around, and this time, she can hear him muttering, "Unbelievable... Odious woman... *Manipulative.*"

But his pace has slowed, noticeably. Diana grins and falls into step with him.

Chapter Three

DIANA

Logan stands before the window, his hands pressed firmly on the wooden paneling as if grounding himself. The world outside is a blur of black glass, his breath fogging the cold surface. Diana watches him, noticing the dusty streaks his palms leave on the pane. But Logan doesn't seem to care. Whatever storm rages outside is nothing compared to the one she can see brewing inside him. His dark eyebrows lift slightly, like he's only just realized how intense the blizzard has become.

Diana steps closer, hesitating for a moment, watching the tension coil in his body. There's a battle waging behind his eyes, something distant and unreachable.

"Do you have something to eat? I could cook for us while we wait," she offers, hoping to break through his walls with a small distraction. His grim smile barely reaches his eyes, but it's something —a small victory. He turns to her and mutters, "Okay."

His hands drop to his sides, and his shoulders slump, resigned. The sight of him looking so defeated tugs at something deep in her chest—guilt, maybe. She tries again, keeping her voice light. "It's fine," she says. "Time will pass. Do you have anything to eat? I could cook for you while we wait."

She considers it a small win, that it gets him to turn around. Even if his smile is mostly grim. "Okay," he says. If she didn't know any better, Diana would have said his smile sprawls a little wider at the sight of her subsequent alarm. She hadn't expected him to agree. All the same, she's glad. She grins encouragingly. His vanishes. *What a difficult man.* "This way," he murmurs. This time, he waits for her to fall in step with him.

The structure of the house doesn't make much sense to her, but Logan moves through it effortlessly. They end up in what can only be the kitchen. The room is vast, and though dark, Diana can sense its old grandeur in the faint outline of the heavy furniture and wide countertops.

Logan pauses near an old wood-burning stove, bending down to open a small compartment. With a flick of a match, the stove crackles to life, casting a soft glow across the room. Eerie shadows play along the walls, and the air grows slightly warmer.

"I didn't think there'd be any heat left in here," she mutters, rubbing her arms against the cold.

Logan gives her a small grin. "The stove's still good. Wood-burning. It keeps this room warm enough."

"What about light?" Diana asks, squinting into the dim corners.

"No electricity," Logan replies. "Just the fire and some lanterns I found. Makes the place feel more like camping," he adds with a shrug.

"This kitchen is bigger than my entire apartment!" Diana exclaims.

"Ditto," Logan says, his voice muffled as he stands near the pantry. When she looks over, he's rummaging through cans and jars, setting them on the counter.

"Canned beans, jerky, some old preserves... looks like we won't starve," Logan says dryly, straightening up.

"Non-perishables, then," Diana jokes, picking up a dusty can of beans. "Guess we won't be having frozen veggies."

"Beats finding a freezer full of spoiled food," Logan mutters, brushing dust off a jar of pickles.

"Wouldn't be your first crime today, would it, Diana?" Logan teases, the warmth in his voice surprising her. She realizes she's standing closer to him than she intended and takes a step back, hoping he doesn't notice. If he does, he doesn't say anything.

"There's not much else here, unless you're into marshmallows," he adds, almost grinning. "Pantry's mostly jerky and sweets."

The thought of Logan eating marshmallows brings an unexpected smile to her face. Somehow, she can't quite picture him with something as soft and sugary as marshmallows.

It might not be much of a conversation, but Logan doesn't completely shut her out. He lets her help, guiding her with clear instructions. She's surprised to find herself enjoying it. Working side by side in the dim light, they prepare the meal over the heavy porcelain countertops and the old, timeworn stove.

Diana handles the sides, heating canned beans over the stove and mixing in what spices they can find in the pantry. Logan disappears briefly, returning with a dusty bottle of wine. He pours her a glass, sliding it over silently before using the rest for cooking.

By the time the meal is ready, it feels almost gourmet to her. She's so hungry, the lack of conversation doesn't bother her. She notices Logan eating quickly, wolfing down the food like he hasn't had a proper meal in weeks. He even relaxes enough to pour himself a glass of wine—something old, with a French label covered in dust.

After the meal, Diana leans back, patting her stomach with a satisfied groan. "I've got to walk this off. You want to come with?"

Logan's face shifts from contentment to uncertainty, but she isn't surprised. Neither is she surprised when he stands and nods slowly. This time, she waits for him in the doorway. Their footsteps echo together down the hallway as they walk side by side.

LOGAN

Dread sits heavy in the pit of his stomach like a rock at the bottom of the lake.

It's nothing he voices to the journalist, of course. All the same, he isn't naive enough to believe she'll miss it. Her eyes, enchanting as they are, also happen to be disquietingly astute.

There is a sense, every time her gaze skims over him, that she sloughs away another layer of his barrier. Keeping several paces of space between them doesn't seem to be doing much.

Unfortunately, he can't stop watching her regardless.

As much as Logan would like to claim the contents of the mansion are already charted territory for him, they aren't. He'd barely gotten through a wing before he'd given up. Still, it's Diana Hayes who is more riveting; a sight of screaming color amidst a backdrop that may as well be monochromatic. It isn't just her physical attributes. Just as detrimental is the way she speaks; direct, animated. "Did you know this place was first built in 1914? I don't know as much about architecture as I'd like to. Do you ever feel that way about stuff? Like there are things you want to know, so many things, but there will never be enough time to know them all?"

It doesn't matter how clipped his responses are, Diana isn't discouraged. She rolls with it. The only saving grace is that she doesn't look right at him while she chatters, so lively. For all the 'Off the record's she's been plugging in, in between questions, for the last half hour... she very much seems more intrigued by the mansion than she does him. That's fortunate.

Logan has to admit that her curiosity reshapes his own perspective a little. It's more difficult than he likes, to remain impervious to the wonder she talks about it with. He's too ensconced to notice how far into the place they have meandered until it's too late. She's already throwing open the door to what has to be the master suite before he can react.

"Woah," Diana blurts. An accurate assessment.

Whatever kind of room it must have once classified as, it has no bed in it now. That isn't anywhere near the most interesting aspect of it. All around them, sketches are pinned—*taped?* He isn't sure—to every conceivable inch of the walls. The person who hung them must have been tall; they are pinned over the six feet and two inches of Logan's height.

Somehow, Diana knows to look at him. He feels it, when she does. Like a feather, tickling, an unignorable nuisance. But Logan doesn't have it in him to feign neutrality. He lets himself be tugged deeper into the room. As if he has a choice about it.

Dust obscures much of the artwork. Some of it, the ink and lead and paint, has faded with time. The floorboards creak under his tread. His heart must not literally fall out, but it feels like it has. He can't fight the premonition burning in his bones: *I know this artist.* Diana's footsteps are much quieter behind him. Not silent, though. He hears her walking. He knows it's towards him.

He doesn't expect what she holds out to him—doesn't understand, even as he finds himself reaching out to accept it. The journal is made of real leather. On first touch against the cool fabric, he knows it. The words distort in front of his eyes. He'd know that handwriting anywhere. He doesn't tell the journalist that. For so many reasons, but above all that he wouldn't know how to.

Logan doesn't plan to hand it back to her. He doesn't foresee, either, the way her lovely voice will fill the room when she reads aloud, "Devereaux Boarding House... 1983. This is the right place. These are the right people. I never understood what people were talking about when they talked about community and rest. This work that I do—my soul's work—is a solitary endeavor. How could rest help? Was not every other peer a competitor? I know now why Delia called it a retreat." The awe that saturates Diana's declamation is transparent.

Logan, grief bruising his heart like a boulder atop his chest, envies it.

Chapter Four

LOGAN

When Logan had been much younger, he'd had a foster brother who'd told him he never realized how hungry he was until he'd finally had something to eat. He remembers the way he'd understood that. He had never been too good with words, and had suffered plenty in consequence for it. It meant twice as much to him for someone to have put into words something Logan never could have.

Logan wondered who had stocked up on so much firewood before the mansion was abandoned. He supposed it was one of the few blessings of this forgotten place. The rough texture of bark against his palms is vivid. It feels good. Achieving something with his hands feels even better.

The way it had, before, in the kitchen. It's been a long time—too long a time, his weary bones protest—since he's created something. But putting a meal together, even if he'd had help, had felt close to the feeling that had once been his norm.

As the fire grows, gnawing at kindling, heating his cheeks until he has feeling back in his face, Logan lets the storm of emotion raise tumult across his face. Diana isn't here. Accepting that the storm wouldn't be letting up tonight, she'd gone to go clean herself up; whatever else this place was lacking, they at least had running water. With a pair of warmer clothes and a thicker coat to match the ridiculous monstrosity still swathed around him, he'd sent her off himself.

In retrospect, he wonders if he ought've known something had stirred in him. Whether it's the familiar task of making something that had been the catalyst, or the journal he hadn't been able to let Diana read too much of, Logan can't say. He doesn't question it. The impulse is fragile as a hummingbird's heartbeat, coaxing him towards a sketchbook he'd packed on sheer whim.

He sketches mindlessly. This, too, feels familiar. It feels like coming home. His head floats, as if right away from his body. His hand takes charge, etching, the graphite nib scratching against the sheet in the most intimate of whispers.

Then there's a creak. Then... *CLANG!* The pencil falls right out of his hand, alarmed, tossed to the wayside with a dull clatter. Diana's scream is unmistakable when it pierces the frigid air. Not a single thought flits through Logan's head.

He's on his feet. He just runs. His heavy-soled boots thwack thunderously down the hallway, skidding with a screech over marble flooring as he races towards her. In hindsight, he probably should have knocked first. In the haze of his panic, he throws the bathroom door open—just to find Diana, and nothing but the endless waterfall of her hair covering her. He turns around so quickly, instinctively, before she even has a chance to shriek; the sight of her disappears in a blur.

"Uh– Crap! Sorry!" Logan sounds strangled even to his own ear. He isn't sure he can breathe. It takes him several minutes to register that he's standing in the middle of a pool of water. The tiles were not only slick, but flooded. "What—?" Baffled, he starts to turn around.

"Logan! Naked here!" Diana shrieks. He can't even enjoy her being the one squawking. His ears, he's certain, are scarlet by now. "Can you—just hand me the towel. Toss it! Don't turn around."

With all the rigidity of a robot, he follows her instructions. Even when she says, "'Kay. You can turn now," he's reluctant to.

"I thought you were in trouble," he grumbles defensively to the wet tile.

"Yeah, I know," she snorts. The sound surprises him enough to jerk his head up to look at her. A choice he regrets immediately after, given her addition of, "But that was enough of a thank you, wasn't it?" It isn't often in life that Logan Black has found himself grateful for the excess melanin of his skin tone. But now, when he can feel heat flush halfway down his chest, he is immeasurably appreciative for the cover it provides.

Even out of peripheral view, he doesn't miss the smile that quirks a corner of her mouth. "Sorry," he says again. "Really."

"A pipe burst," Diana explains, moving briskly, determined to stay on task. Logan doesn't bother looking up, but he can hear the shuffle of her movements—like she's trying to fix something. The uncomfortable truth gnaws at him: he's a man, she's a woman, and they're alone in this abandoned, eerie mansion. No matter how much he resents her being here, Logan can't shake the instinct to avoid doing anything that might make her feel unsafe.

But then, the sharp sound of fabric tearing jolts him. "What—?" He spins around, his voice hoarse. Diana, thankfully, is still fully clothed, bundled in a coat much like his own. Somehow, she's rigged a torn piece of fabric to tie around the leaking pipe, slowing the water to a mere drip.

"We don't want the water to keep running, do we?" she says, her tone entirely practical. "Now, I just need to find the main valve and shut it off before the entire place floods. This mansion has such strong bones, Logan. It would be tragic if something that has stood the test of time so well were ruined by something as ordinary as water damage."

Logan opens his mouth to reply—then shuts it again. He's at a loss for words, captivated by how this strange, remarkable woman moves with such purpose.

"Can I come with you?" he asks at last, the words escaping before he can second-guess them.

He doesn't need to look up to see her smile. "Careful, Mr. Black. Or I might just think you're starting to like me." She says it playfully, but there's something genuine in her voice. Logan glances up anyway.

"Come on," he says, gesturing for her to lead the way.

Much to his astonishment, Diana doesn't say much as they begin another trek through the mansion. She's eerily quiet. If he'd thought her chattering unnerved him, Logan doesn't have any words for how her silence feels. He only knows it doesn't comfort him. He makes it down two hallways before he breaks. Attempting teasing, he quips, "What, are you finally out of questions?"

"No," Diana answers seriously. "I'm just – still thinking about that journal."

The journal in question is still in his back pocket. Folded in on itself, like a letter tucked away. At her mention of it, it burns its presence. It's so dark here, he couldn't pull it out to read. He pulls it out to feel its weight in his hand. It's so much heavier than she knows.

Logan makes a choice without deciding. "I'll tell you something," he says. "Off the record."

DIANA

Diana stills at his offer. Not even in her wildest dreams could she have predicted these words would leave Logan's mouth. But evidence that they have is splayed all over his face. He looks stunned himself.

For a long moment, she isn't sure he hasn't changed his mind. He hasn't said anything. He looks, actually, like Rachel's little boy, Jamie, does when he's doing his math homework. They keep walking. She ducks her head into rooms here and there, but it's always the wrong one. Mostly, she's seeing without seeing. She's all too aware of his body beside hers. Of the gears turning in his head, loudly.

"I had a mentor," Logan says, his voice taut, barely above a whisper. "It's his journal... his drawings." The words seemed to weigh him down as if they had been trapped inside for too long. Diana feels the chill in the air shift, replaced by the gravity of his confession. "August Laurier," he continues, finally exhaling a breath he'd been holding for years.

Diana nods slowly, recognition flickering in her mind. She shoves her hands into her pockets, absorbing the weight of what he had just shared. This isn't just about art—it's about the pieces of himself Logan has lost along the way.

Logan looks at her like he's waiting for her to say something. So, she asks him: "Where do I know that name from, Logan?"

It's the first time she's heard him laugh. Even in the videos of him online, Logan always looked so somber. This sound is mirthless. As it permeates the air between them, the air feels too thick. It's like it was pressing down on her. His answer does nothing to alleviate it when he replies, "Gus was my mentor. He was one of the most decorated impressionist artists of the twenty-first century. *Had* a mentor. Was, Diana. Past tense. He passed away two years ago. With him, so went my so-called mojo."

The universe has a cruel sense of humor. No sooner has Logan offered her this confession that they come upon a large, heavy-looking door—back inside the kitchen of all places. Exasperation colors her voice as she huffs, "Does this place have a basement? A – a cellar, maybe?"

Logan answers distractedly, "Yeah, of course. That's where I got the wine from." If she isn't mistaken, however, and Diana doesn't believe she is, she could swear the artist looks *relieved* by her lack of reaction. It had been an instinctive choice; one, if she's being honest, driven by pure shock. There's more he can say, just within reach. So obviously, in fact, that Diana could liken it to pretending not to see a badly hidden child during a game of hide and seek, despite the feet visible beneath the curtain's trim.

Yet she can't fight the hunch that he isn't ready. Her arm hooks through his, taking a liberty when he's the one who's opened the portal to it. *In for a penny, in for a pound* as they say. Logan relaxes into the contact quickly enough that she doesn't comment on his momentary stiffness. It counts for something, that he doesn't pry himself out of her hold.

"Do you see anything?" he asks nervously, descending the stairs slowly.

"Yes, actually," Diana answers cheerfully. "Right there—do you see? That's a valve. We just... Hold on–" She gently pulls free of his hold and weaves her way through what must be the utility room. The water heater, though relatively new, is coated in dust. Right beside it, she finds a valve made of brass, its wheel-shaped handle slightly rusted but still functional. She grips it and twists. With a creak, the water slows, the sound fading into a final trickle before stopping completely.

"Got it," she announces.

She turns back with a bright, victorious grin. Just as she's about to boast, though—her eyes follow Logan's line of sight. Against the wall opposite, several shovels are propped up. She looks at him. In the dark of the basement, Logan looks back at her. She hadn't thought they were standing so close anymore. She can taste his breath, though; the sour-sweet loveliness of wine lingering. He says nothing. His pinched brows look troubled. "Logan?" Diana murmurs gently. Her palm comes to rest against his chest, to urge him from his reverie.

"Diana," he says. She can feel the syllables of her name vibrate in his chest. *Oh.*

She has to swallow before her cottoned mouth can suggest, "This could be an opportunity, you know." Glass half-full kind of woman that she is, Diana can't help it. "This journal... It's something you can learn from, about someone you lost too soon. It won't bring him back, and it may not alleviate any of your grief, but – something is better than nothing, isn't it? I was never great with numbers, but that's still true." Her knuckles knock against his chest like it's a door. "Right?"

Somehow, she makes him laugh again. This time, it isn't so bitter a sound. It lodges a lump the size of a tennis ball in her throat. "I'm dyslexic. I never dealt with it. So, I can't read too well. And yeah, I get how ironic this is."

She feels it bubbling up her throat, her laughter, before she can even think of staunching it. She can't help it. It spills over, with such a force her body almost keels over into his. Quickly, but earnestly, she offers, "I can read it to you! I mean, obviously, if you don't mind me reading it with you. Off—"

"—the record," Logan finishes. His eyes roll, but not unkindly. She'll take it. "Of course. Fine." If his laughter was disconcerting, not even Diana's extensive vocabulary affords her a word for what Logan's smile does to her. It's such a wild thing, baring his teeth. His eyes scrunch almost all the way shut. Like a magic trick, he looks a decade younger. It's an untarnished, kid's smile.

It makes her itch to divulge her secrets to him. Over pinky promises in the sandbox. So, she confesses, "I'm not trying to manipulate you by telling you this, first off. Okay? Remember that. But I've been burnt out, too. My mojo's nowhere to be found. I was just trying to... find something meaningful, I guess? This – Something about *this* felt, *still feels,* meaningful."

Tentatively, but still, Logan lays his hand over the one she rests over his chest. His head is bowed as he whispers, "Me too." His breath is warmer than it ought to be in such a freezing cold space. His eyes are a much lighter, more glacial blue than she'd thought. They turn glassy, and her chest aches. "Or at least to find meaning in my art again. When Gus died, it – it was out of nowhere. He was... He was pretty young. Sixty. Sixty isn't that old, is it? But he was sick. And he didn't tell me."

His smile is lost now. His bottom lip quivers. "I was the one who found him collapsed, though. In his studio. He – Before he went, that day, he told me that what he'd spent his life thinking mattered just didn't. To not make the mistakes he had. That... it's the nature of life, to give up some things to make space for others. That I was great, but greatness has a price. To be *mindful*." The way he says that word, it drips with disgust. Distress, too, Diana thinks. Her hand squeezes his. His voice is brittle when he says, "Nothing I make feels good enough now. Since."

There are so many things she can say.

So many that come to the tip of her tongue, then die there. She's good at talking, she knows that. Words are her thing; they always have been. But she's also not half-bad at intuiting what people need. Right then, she just knows, deep in her bones, that Logan Black doesn't need her wisdom. He needs an ear to listen. He needs a *friend*. Most of all, he needs someone to wrap their arms around him and squeeze him tightly, to smooth a hand over his head, and let him unravel.

So, she gives him that.

Chapter Five

DIANA

With that first sharp inhale as she comes to, Diana's senses are flooded with the rich, earthy aroma of what is, unmistakably, freshly brewed coffee. The warm scent earns a deep-seated groan from the back of her throat. Though, fine, maybe that's partly from stretching her stiff limbs on the chaise longue she must've fallen asleep reading on.

"Good morning, sunshine." Logan's voice, deep and warm, matches the aroma of the coffee filling the room. His words stir her from sleep, the weight of the night before lingering in her thoughts.

Her eyes flutter open, focusing on the cherry-red mug he holds out to her. Over the rim, his eyes—winter-cold, but softened by the morning light—hold a tenderness that catches her off guard. Logan isn't just handsome; there is something raw, something real beneath the surface that takes her breath away.

"Hi," she croaks, stunned by his willful proximity.

She knew they'd made progress the evening before. She hadn't anticipated it having been this big of a leap forward. However, evidence to the contrary splays itself all over Logan's face. There is a softness there now, where a shuttered-off vacancy had been. "Hi," he confirms. "I woke up in the mood for cereal. The seriously sugary, probably bad for you kind. Poured it out into bowls and everything —" His head jerks to the side, where, on top of an intricately carved table sits a heavy-looking tray, with a cup that must be Logan's exuding wisps of steam, and two bowls full of cereal but no, "—and found out there was no milk, right after. So, how do you feel about coffee and dry cereal?"

Diana can't help but giggle at the wide-eyed earnestness he looks at her with. How much difference, she marvels, acts of kindness made. They could be so healing. "Let me brush my teeth," she suggests, gratefully accepting the mug he's still holding out to her, "and then I'm on board. That stuff's usually reserved for midnight binges for me, but I'll make an exception."

"Time is a social construct," Logan agrees sagely. Diana manages not to burst into laughter over it. "Do you have a toothbrush?"

"My big sister, Audrey, always said you should always have a change of underwear, wet wipes, a toothbrush, and a pocket knife in your purse," she parrots, "so I do." Despite her sour, fuzzy-tasting mouth, she still sips the coffee. Heat spreads through her chest immediately. She has to take another one. "God, that's *so good*. Thank you." Logan's eyes scrunch on the sides from the proud smile that curls his lips. It's adorable.

As the warmth—of the coffee, yes, but more concerningly, Logan's sweetened disposition—settles around her, prickling guilt sticks out like a sore thumb. His open-faced tenderness is to blame. How can she accept it, no strings attached, when they both know why she had come here? The thought of taking advantage of Logan's vulnerability sits acidly at the back of her throat. Diana is left with no choice. She blurts, "I – Uh, there were shovels. In the cellar?" She had to speak up. She *had to*. She knows it. "If you're amenable to helping me out, you know, I could be out of your hair in a couple of hours."

To her astonishment, Logan only shakes his head. "Don't be stupid, it's still snowing, Diana," he dismisses without pause. She can only blink at him. Logan, as if he doesn't notice it, simply says, "Besides, if you read more to me today... I'll even let you use my toothpaste."

Her eyes drift to the journal she'd fallen asleep with. It sits heavily atop her thighs now. She can see where one of them must have dog-eared the corner of the page they'd left off. They were a quarter of the way through—Diana pronouncing art techniques that went right over her head, but that Logan listened to, riveted. He'd still taken the time to explain each one to her. Handling his syllables with care, as if they were colors he was choosing for a canvas of his own. It had been nice to see that she hadn't assumed wrong, after all. 'Moody' could still be conflated with 'passionate' when it came to an artist; this artist in particular.

She nods to him. "Okay," she agrees. He grins at her winningly. Diana lets him pretend he didn't know her answer would be a Yes all along.

"He's funny. Was he this funny at sixty?" Diana asks, looking up from the journal lest she walk into one of the marbles – again. She doesn't think too hard about the hand that rests at the small of her back, already catering towards preventing it.

They're walking around the mansion again. After Logan had admitted he hadn't explored much of the place on his own in the two weeks he'd been here, Diana had demanded they remedy the travesty immediately. With makeshift morning routines and a surprisingly satisfying breakfast out of the way, they wandered whimsically with August's weathered journal flipped back open to where they'd last left off,.

They take breaks throughout the day, lingering in one room or another. Exploring architecture, with so many stories covered in dust but not undone by it. She can see something in Logan stir, though she's careful not to call attention to it. Still, it means something to her. To get to witness the delicate reverence with which his fingertips skim over details. The way his brow furrows, like he's trying to commit it to memory.

Diana doesn't blame him. The estate in the broad light of day is something else entirely.

"He was funny, yeah," Logan tells her. "It was even better because he didn't look it. Extremely severe features; a stern, almost angry brow. Prone to being romanticized by no end of grad students, but the man didn't give off 'Come, I'll make you laugh till you cry' energy."

Diana's head whips sideways to shoot him a pointed glance. "Unlike you, obviously."

Logan rolls his eyes. There's no acerbity to it, though. The corners of his lips are quirked, albeit gently. "No," he says casually, "very much like me. At least the face. Not the jokes or the grad students."

"Not even *one?*" Diana asks, suspicious and disbelieving.

She wouldn't have thought him capable of it if she weren't witnessing it now, but his grin manages to be startlingly *impish*. He relents, "Fine. Maybe one... or two. But definitely not the jokes." She honestly can't tell if the man is joking or not. The idea of it, however, has her biting the inside of her cheek, her jaw clenching at the thought of him smiling like this at someone else.

"Yeah," Diana harrumphs, "you're not very funny, nope."

"What's one more failing? Maybe that's what I'll be a professional at next." Logan surrenders too easily. She can't decide if it bothers her more that he doesn't even sound bothered by the prospect, or that he drops his hand from its place on her back to flap beside him as he shrugs. Probably, she's thinking too much.

She goes right back to reading.

. . .

LOGAN

Before they know it, it's dark outside again.

This time they switch roles in the kitchen. Diana takes over the protein—heating up canned beef with dried herbs and spices she found in the pantry, mixing it into a rich broth. Logan handles the rest, tossing some jerky and canned beans into the pot to thicken the stew. They work with what they have, and soon enough, a hearty stew is bubbling over the wood-burning stove. The smell of savory meat and spices fills the air.

When they're done, they carry mismatched bowls, brimming with the chunky stew, to settle in front of the hearth on a sheet they've spread out. It's not gourmet, but it feels like a feast—a makeshift picnic in the dim glow of the firelight.

It warms Logan's chest in a way that has nothing to do with the fire, the absolute astonishment contorting Diana's fairy features when he suggests it. But it's her who suggests they keep reading. She doesn't bring up leaving again. That doesn't stop it from being the elephant in the room. No matter how cozy it is, to curl up in the warmth of one another's companionship, there is a time limit on this. Diana has a life outside of this. She may be burnt out – but she isn't lost the way he is. Logan isn't unaware of that.

Fortunately, it's old hat for him.

So much of art is about capturing a moment in time—maybe even just a *feeling* at a moment in time. Diana definitely inspires those. He watches her, ladling spoonfuls into her mouth in between the excerpts she reads with inflections to her voice that betray a background in theater. It almost dilutes the grief that keeps threatening to crawl up his throat in waves of nausea every time he thinks about it. About Gus. About the differences between the man whose thoughts she reads aloud with gravitas, and the one whose heart Logan had watched stop. *Almost.* But not quite.

"– Logan?" Her voice pierces his haze like an arrow through a cloud of fog. His head jerks back out of the palm that had been cradling his jaw.

"I'm fine," he says defensively, automatically.

Diana frowns at him. "Please don't lie to me." Her words are clipped, almost curt. Dread becomes a weight on his chest, the blood in his veins replaced with quicksilver.

"I'm not," he argues. "You can keep reading."

"I know I can. I don't want to," Diana retorts. It is the first time he has heard her voice turn sharp. He can't help but ricochet back to when she had first shown up at the door. The first words she had said to him: *You're an awfully hard man to reach.* How he had thought her voice, so sweet, warm, was what it looked like would come out of her. Charming, pleasantly surprising predictability. Comforting.

He has no right to feel whiplashed when that changes. He has known her for forty-eight hours. *You knew Gus for six years,* a fickle voice sounds at the back of his head. Logan pushes his stew away with stony petulance. "Shouldn't you be glad?" he demands. "I haven't been saying 'off the record.' You've got plenty for a juicy story. You'll break it big in no time, and then you don't have to slum it with a has-been just so you feel less like a loser." Bitterness floods his mouth. His words drip with it. Of course it would leave behind a taste.

Diana just looks at him. Almost as if she's waiting—waiting for him to take it back. To reach out, and snatch the words out of the air. Logan can't. "I didn't deserve that," she whispers furiously. Her hands are quivering fists at her sides. She is on her knees, taller than him like this. Sat prostrate, and still more powerful than him. There's a metaphor here. Logan can't stomach deciphering it.

"If people only ever got what they deserved, we would live in a very different world, Diana," he says hoarsely. "You're a journalist. You know what the world really is."

Logan discovers that color suffuses her porcelain skin when she's angry. Far more than it drenches her words. It's so much worse, that her words leave slaked in tears that cling to her lashes, dampening blonde to visibility, "Except I wasn't trying to be a journalist. I was trying to be your friend. And friends... Care about you enough to tell you when you're being a coward—"

"*Don't,*" Logan spits, recoiling. Stung.

"No. No, *listen,*" she insists, no matter how much his head shakes. Her hands are on his. He can't cover his ears, and he's too fraught with too much to be embarrassed of the overwhelming urge to. "I'm not on my deathbed, but my wisdom should hold some weight. And I'm telling you that you're not a has-been. You're hurt. And sometimes, licking wounds isn't all it takes to heal them. Sometimes... Sometimes, you need stitches, Logan. It's *okay* for everything to not be beautiful. If you look with the right perspective, there could be poetry in anything."

Logan wrenches his hands away from her. "I *said* don't. Why can't you just– Just *leave it alone,* Diana! I'm not a poet. I'm—"

"What?" she demands, pushing. "You're *what,* Logan?"

His body is cold. So cold. "Done," he says. He doesn't move, watching her walk away. He doesn't do anything at all.

Chapter Six

LOGAN

The parlor only grows colder in her absence. Logan finds it isn't a totally sentimental observation when he can see the fire dying, too. Too much weighs his bones down. He doesn't move to feed more wood to the flames. Instead, he watches it die in what must be slow-motion. Tragedy, Logan has realized, comes too swiftly or the absolute opposite. Whichever direction it chose, it obliterated laws of nature. It had a nature of its own.

Only a prying spectator could admire that without resenting it. And resentment could only keep a man warm for so long. The bitter chill seeps in past layers of heavy fabric and flayed-feeling flesh. "Can't get any worse than this," he mutters to himself, flopping backwards on the ground with a hefty thump.

A low grumble sounds as if from a distance. His palms splay on top of the floorboard; he feels the vibration. The glass crystals of the chandelier catch brief flashes of lightning through the windows, casting eerie reflections on the walls. He flinches with his whole body when the first flash swallows the room in blinding light.

Just like that, the mansion is plunged in absolute darkness. Every shadow is in stark relief; his body prone amidst the spindly bones of decrepit furniture. Flakes must morph to shapeless chunks of ice, the way they pelt against the window. The wind wails mournfully, rattling the window frames like the bars of a prison cell.

The storm rages outside, furious and relentless, battering the mansion with a force that mirrors the chaos inside Logan's chest. He can't move. It isn't just the storm pressing in on him—it's everything he's been holding back. The memories...flood in uninvited, as overwhelming as the wind howls against the windows.

He's been here before—lost in the same suffocating void. Not in this room, but in this feeling, this grief that refused to let him go.

Diana's heavy boots muffle the chaos raging outside. She's on her knees, crouched by his head, before he can even process what's gone on. He doesn't understand that his tears have spilled until her hands are on his cheeks. His breath turns shallow, his whisper brittle, asking, "I thought – you were mad at me?"

Her sigh is warm. He thinks of the blow dryer he and his foster siblings had used one Thanksgiving to try and melt the turkey they had stolen out of a rich woman's idling trolley. His stomach grumbles. "I'm not mad," she murmurs, her hand stroking his cheek. "I'm frustrated. That doesn't mean I don't still care about you."

Diana's revelation is untouched by pride. She says the words so solidly, there is no room for doubt to slither in. Something inside of him thaws, like the frigid cold once the hearth is ablaze in all its glory. "Thank you," he breathes.

"Of course," she exhales back, her head bowing to press her forehead to his. Her breath is hot when she presses her lips to the crown of his head.

"Can I—?" he begins. Regretful about it, when she pulls back to look at him somberly. "Can I show you something?"

She gives him a brief nod, and the tiniest of smiles. It isn't much, but it is everything.

With a squeeze of her hand, Logan scrambles to his feet. He rushes to fetch it, wondering if this is how dogs feel, bringing their beloved owners newspapers first thing in the mornings. The way that they did in cartoons. Would his tail wag, thumping excitedly against the floorboards? There is no way to know. But his heart pounds maniacally in his chest as he holds the offering out to her. A canvas. *His* canvas – or the one he'd come across and claimed as his own. His signature is already sitting in the bottom right corner, like a talisman.

He doesn't need to see it. Isn't totally ready to, actually.

Then, Diana throws her arms around his neck.

DIANA

Simple contact may as well be lightning. It strikes in the moment Logan's arms encircle her, reeling her closer. His palm rests at her nape, fingers carded through frizzy tendrils till his icy fingers are against her skin. The cold isn't the only reason a shiver wracks through Diana's body.

"Do you like it?" he asks against the shell of her ear.

There is a lump in Diana's throat and she doesn't trust herself to speak around it. It's etched in her mind already, the cursory sketch he'd done of her. Fine lines, bolder strokes, and stunning shading. It was a beginning. It was... Oh, it was everything.

"Being your muse?" she asks, her laughter wet and choked. "Yes. I'm honored." It takes a profound amount of willpower to unspool her limbs from around him. With her hands on his shoulders, she takes the moment to look him in the eye. "Does this mean what I think it means?" she asks, breath bated.

His head ducks, unable to meet her eyes. Avoiding her, it looks like. Diana understands him perfectly, at that moment. Logan isn't moody or cold. He's just – shy. He isn't a coward, either. That, he proves to both of them, adamantly puffing his chest to ask her: "Will you sit for me?"

Diana can taste the fondness her beaming mouth effuses. "We should find some candles," she says. Her hand slips into his, as if it had been his idea to hold them. Somehow, she suspects he will like that. She doesn't have to look at him to feel him smiling. She squeezes his hand, leading him through the sprawling estate she's already managed to make an impressive amount of sense of.

It doesn't hurt, when his brows flick halfway up his forehead, visibly impressed, end up in the same master suite this had all begun. "Here?" she invites. Testing him, maybe. Still a little sore from his abrasiveness, risen above but not yet forgotten.

He raises her knuckles to his startlingly warm mouth. The kiss he presses to the bones is as delicate as his nod. "Will you talk to me?"

She does not know Logan very well, technically – not from the source, at least. She's managed to wrangle from him some facts, of course. The way he identifies his own art style as somewhere between the dramatic tension of Baroque and the emphatic, dynamic movement and light of Impressionism. He doesn't have a favorite color. It would be unfair to the others; each one had its uses. He thought almost everyone in America pretending to like pizza was a cultural choice, not because they actually liked the taste. He preferred to watch movies in black and white, because otherwise the color distracted him. Oh, and that he couldn't paint in silence.

Of all the things he had brought along with them, his iPod hadn't been one of them. His phone is at the bottom of his duffle bag, dead. There can be no music. "You need me to be your noise," she summarizes.

Logan pivots on his heel, halting in search of whatever instruments he sees fit for his endeavor. "No," he denies with force. "I just – no. I just like the sound of your voice. I like... hearing about your life."

He puts it so earnestly, she doesn't think of denying him. She prefaces, admitting to him outright that she isn't often on the other side of the interviews. She'd never met a question she didn't enjoy, so long as it was coming from her lips. She didn't think she was good at talking about herself. She did acknowledge that the way she enjoyed wireframing conversations had something to do with the control it offers. All the same, she tells him—then surrenders the control.

Maybe it's the exhaustion she can thank. But her mouth starts running, and she just lets it. She tells him she's originally from New Jersey, born and raised. She had gone to NYU for a degree in Journalism, always clear on what she had wanted. It hadn't been a step-by-step plan so much as it had been a mental image she climbed rungs towards. She had been on assignment for an internship that paid a measly pittance when she had come to Maplewood Grove. Doing a fluff piece on quintessential small towns for a weekend getaway. She had fallen in love with it at first glance.

She explains the way being a big fish in a small pond had sounded amazing to her. She cops to her arrogance in overestimating the way the amount of opportunities in a fishbowl would feel, years down the line.

But she also tells him about her life. Not just her work, but – her friends. Her girls. The book club she had joined on impulse, having walked into her darling pal Patty Sullivan's woo-woo bookstore, practically bursting with all the worldly memorabilia she'd stuffed the place with. She gushes about Maggie, and the way her first love had come back around. She explains the way Rachel is so different from her, but in knowing her, she's grown up more than she'd expected. She talks about Izzie, and how she'd never really had adult friendships like this before, so full of support and tenderness.

The smell of paint and turpentine perfume the stories. Diana pours, and Logan paints.

She must drift off, somewhere in the night. Maybe hours have passed—but the storm feels farther now, distant as a nightmare from the night before. In the haze between slumber and wakefulness, she registered another layer being spread over her collapsed body. His lips press to her forehead, breath tickling her cheeks.

In the end, it just happens: as unconscious as it isn't, the upwards cant of her soft chin. His lips meet hers. The last thing she clings to before sleep tugs her under is: he tastes like marshmallows after all.

Chapter Seven

WHEN DIANA AWAKENS, there is a heavy weight atop her thighs. The coat he had slipped off and tossed over her supine body like a blanket, she had expected. A second one, not to mention a man's head—oh, *Logan*'s head—in her lap is a surprise.

Her head lifts to find he's sat on the ground. He isn't asleep. From where he is curled up, parallel to where her own head had slumped back, rests a finished painting. Diana doesn't need to touch it to know the paint is still wet. He must not have finished it too long ago.

With slender fingers coaxing his face to hers, Diana doesn't know what she will find on his face. Her heart soars over what she does: a brilliant grin that's overtaken his features, and tears in his eyes. His exhausted eyes, but that proud mouth. His voice is as much velvet as it is gravel as he says, "You made me feel again." Tears prick her own eyes, unbidden. "I'll do your interview, Diana."

Her jaw drops. Diana sits up so fast—too fast—and vertigo strikes vehemently, making her head spin. Still, she protests, "You don't have to. I don't want you to do this because you feel *indebted* to me or something. That isn't why I did this. I promise you."

Much to her astonishment, Logan chuckles. "I know. But what if I want to do it anyway?"

Diana's words leave thickly: "Oh."

"But will you take me back to your town, first? Maybe buy me some breakfast? I am officially a starving artist again," he teases.

Her nod is as earnest as the emotion in every line of Logan's face. "I would love that."

Together, hand in hand, they finally return to the shovels they had left in the mansion's basement two days ago. Each of them grabs one each, and they brave the cold together. They shovel Diana's car out of its frosty prison. When Logan exclaims as much, Diana's giggle melts snowflakes with its warmth. "There's a metaphor there," she says.

"Yeah. You're sunshine."

"And you said you aren't a poet." Her tongue clucks, and her hands plant on either side of her waist in faux reprimand.

Logan shrugs, unrepentant.

Diana asks him, dropping into the driver's seat. "Are you ready for the real world again?"

It doesn't surprise her that Logan quiets. He takes the moment, and she's glad to give it to him. She fiddles with the car's heater— accepting it is no freshly blazing fire, but it will do. Logan still takes her hand in his. "I think that's what Gus meant," he says. "Maybe the point is to let the world in instead of hiding away to document it. The colors flood in that way. The drowning may burn my lungs, fine – but isn't it so worth it anyway?"

Diana's smile is undeniably smug. It's a gorgeous sight, if a confusing one. "Why?" Logan prompts, a brow arching in question.

It's her turn to shrug now. "I was right, is all. About artists being passionate. You, a poet."

Logan sighs. "When inspired, my angel," he allows.

98

Out of their makeshift time-capsule, there is only one place Diana can think to take a freshly resuscitated man: *Loretta's Diner*. It's waffles that the journalist thinks the artist has earned. Instead, when she shoves open the door, dinging her presence, it is chaos she discovers.

Sheriff Colton Rhodes' uniform jacket is unmistakable from the back. What is startling is the way half the *town* seems to be sequestered around his table, ranting together and apart, too many voices overlapping. Patty's voice is immediately distinguishable. The breezy, whimsical woman loses her eternal cool so rarely, it stuns Diana. Though just as alarming are her girls – Maggie, distraught; Rachel, pale with concern; Izzie, ruddy-cheeked with fury.

It takes her a solid few seconds to grasp it is *her* name being tossed around.

With her fingers entangled with Logan's, tugging him along, she approaches them. Cautious, but unafraid. "Uh, hello?" Diana intones, baffled.

One could hear a hairpin drop in the silence that takes over. For just a moment—and then, the noise explodes anew. Several bodies fling themselves at her, almost jostling her hand out of Logan's hold. Someone sobs in her ear: "We thought you'd been had by a serial killer, Diana Hayes!"

Well, Real World, Diana thinks, *meet Logan Black*. Out loud, she introduces: "Oh! Oh no, no, no, I – I found a man. This is Logan. He's—" Diana quickly realizes she hasn't thought this through.

Logan bolsters himself to intercept: "Courting the sensational Diana Hayes and building a sanctuary for creativity at the edge of town – in a mansion my dearest friend left me." His hand squeezes around hers.

All around them, in peripheral view, dubious glances are exchanged. Diana thinks she even catches Rachel's little boy sharing one with Max Bennett. It thrills her, she must admit. Even more, when her gaze lands on Logan's—and he only has eyes for her.

The End.

Sweet Blossom

A SMALL TOWN SINGLE MOM BILLIONAIRE
ROMANCE

Chapter One

RACHEL

"Rachel, hon, we're sorry, but with all the budget cuts and fewer kids enrolled, we just can't keep you," the daycare owner says with a sigh, pity etched into the creases around her eyes. "There just isn't enough demand for a third childcare assistant."

Rachel knows when to brace herself. She holds her breath, willing herself to stay composed. The disappointment is familiar, like a constant shadow lurking just behind her. The moment feels inevitable, yet it still hurts like an unexpected blow—another crack in the fragile foundation of her fresh start.

"It came down to seniority," the woman adds apologetically. The unspoken truth hangs heavy between them: last one in, first one out.

"I understand." Rachel tucks a loose strand of strawberry blonde hair behind her ear, forcing out a smile that feels brittle. "Thank you for the opportunity." The words taste hollow, but they come out smooth, practiced.

She moves on autopilot, methodically checking for her phone, grabbing her jacket and purse. The glass door clicks shut behind her.

Twenty minutes ago, this had been her job. Her plan. Now? It's gone.

That isn't the case anymore.

A sharp spring breeze pushes through Maplewood Grove's town square, but it does nothing to lift the weight that sits heavy on Rachel's shoulders. Everything feels surreal, like she's drifting through a bad dream she can't wake from. But the dread curling in her stomach is all too real. She hates how familiar it's become—this feeling of uncertainty, teetering on the edge of failure. For a moment, she wishes she could be angry, but all she feels is... tired.

Anger feels powerful. Anger is what strong people feel. But what she feels? This sinking, embarrassing feeling? It's useless. Familiar, but never easier.

Rachel checks her phone again, though she knows better. No missed calls. No messages. Just silence. The daycare had been her best hope—a way to settle into something steady. Now, even that plan is gone. She needs something more than hope. She needs a job. A future. Something concrete to rely on.

Rachel has a little boy to think of, who's her whole world.

With Jamie at school and no job to rush off to, though, the day stretches out before her—but not with possibility. It's empty and uncertain. Daunting. She has to force herself to take the same measured, deep breaths she makes Jamie take when he's scared. Among so many other, more adult worries, that's what she is. Just plain old little kid scared.

It makes her want to curl up in a ball under her mother's dining table, the way she used to with her dad when she was a little girl afraid of thunderstorms because their dog was. Except, for so many reasons, she can't.

Only the first of which is that she *isn't* a little kid. She's the opposite: a mom. A single mom, at that, though whose fault that is isn't an argument that's been won in any direction yet. The truth stings:

she's thirty-two with little job experience beyond managing chaos, keeping things together, and nurturing others. Maybe that's the price of falling headfirst in love right out of college with a man who seemed solid and capable, only to realize how quickly things can unravel.

Meanwhile, her parents had sold their home, the one Rachel and all three of her older sisters had grown up in, a couple of years ago and taken off to travel the world in their RV. Their life is one big adventure; the two of them have already grown old together, built a marriage worthy of pride, and are still very much in love with each other. It stings, on her darker days—that they have that, and she can't even bear to tell them they're sending their sweet little postcards to the wrong mailing address. Even that, there's an hourglass running out on; it's trickling time until they stop someplace for long enough to be reachable to someone other than their kids, and find out she's in town from Maplewood Grove's grapevine.

Her chest tightens just thinking about it. Still, her feet carry her forward, mindlessly, past the general store and Sunrise Bakery. Whether it's muscle memory from what feels like a lifetime ago, or Maplewood being so unchanged and simple, Rachel isn't sure. It could be a little of both. She lingers in front of painted storefronts and quaint facades, scanning for some **HELP WANTED**! or **NOW HIRING!** signs. Uselessly, she already knows; if anyone was hiring, the news would've already spread.

Some things, she thinks, walking past the flower shop she'd worked in after school as a teenager, *never change.* It's as comforting as it is the opposite. She looks in through windows and, native or not, she may as well be an outsider. There's an ease between the rest of them, and Rachel can't even place the last time she experienced something akin to that. The appeal of this simplicity—the routine, predictability, and unharried, timeless charm—is the most solid ground beneath her feet. Yet it's so... *set.*

She can't seem to break through. Or to get a real grip, when the rug keeps being pulled out from under her every time she lets herself begin to breathe.

Just like it happens now: in the distance, the school bell rings its sharp, clear trill, slicing through Rachel's reverie like a hot knife through butter. In minutes, Maplewood's calm is punctured by the clamor of what might be every kid in town bursting from school doors at once.

The view is already obscured by the flock of parents and care-takers gathered like a cloud outside. As if envious of the frenzy, the cool breeze surges too. Rachel tugs on her jacket, cinching it around herself, her steps quickening and body weaving a path through the barricade.

And then, there he is. Jamie spots her only a second behind—and runs across the playground that very moment. His fire engine red backpack bounces against his little body when he bounds towards her waiting arms. Nothing could ever beat the unbridled excitement that lights up his face. For a moment in time, every bad feeling in her body melts away. She drops to her knees, just as he collides with her, bursting into snuffling little giggles when she squeezes him, raining kisses on his precious face.

"Mama! Mama, we made *rockets* today! *Real* ones!" he babbles, soft, chubby palms smacking her shoulders giddily. "Well, not *real* ones... but Mr. Forrest did say ours flew highest!"

"No *way*," Rachel gasps with all the elevated, theatrical enthu-siasm she can. "Bud, that's awesome! I'm so proud of you!"

When she stands, her warm, brown eyes—her own mom's eyes—look up at her in his face; his are the best rendition so far, still brim-ming joy and innocence Rachel needs him to keep forever. He beams at her, missing a tooth. Rachel laughs and means it. *Jamie,* she thinks, nodding along to his chatter, recapping his day in granular detail, starting their walk home, his steps half-skipped. *Jamie is the one good thing. This is why I can't fail—I can't fail either of us. There has to be something in town. There has to be.*

It's almost a prayer sent out to the universe, from the bottom of her heart.

MAX

His life isn't a perfect repetition of the same day, but it's not much of a departure either. That's the rhythm of life in Maplewood Grove. The path to the Whispering Willow is one Max knows by heart. As soon as he steps inside, the aroma of dark roast coffee and aged books envelops him—an unexpected burst of autumn sweetness amid the spring air. Max inhales deeply, letting the scent settle at the base of his lungs, grounding him in a familiar comfort.

"Maxwell, my sweet," Patty Sullivan greets, as bright and lively as ever, leaning on her elbows over the counter. The bookstore-slash-café owner defies what most people picture when they think of an entrepreneur in Maplewood Grove. But then, Patty's always been a rare gem in town, much like her shop, brimming with mementos from a life so vivid that Max often wonders why she keeps coming back to the quiet comfort of home. On the other hand, she asks him: "Same as always?"

She's radiant and keen; an instantaneous, vehement contrast to the bone-deep exhaustion he knows he exudes. Patty, bless her, doesn't point it out.

"Yeah, you know it," Max says sheepishly. She accepts it, waiting for him to confirm before she launches into fixing his flat white, though they both know she doesn't have to. He shoots her a small smile for it. The weight of the day lifts off his chest by a pound or two.

The coffee machine hisses and Patty asks, "Busy day?"

Max runs a hand through his air, hip leaning against the counter. "Slow one," he answers. "Those are the crap ones. Busy is good. But you know how that is."

Patty laughs with her whole chest. "I wouldn't know what that's like," she teases, brows arching pointedly at the gaggle of women arguing back and forth amidst a chorus of laughter in the background.

He chuckles, his head shaking. "You never want to join?"

"She's more into entertainment than analysis," a deeper, gristlier voice sounds behind Max. He doesn't have to turn to know it's Sheriff Colton Rhodes. Still, he does pivot halfway to raise a hand in hello. The other man is older and shorter, but he takes up space the same way Patty does. Firm, and cool as a cucumber. "What he said," Patty agrees, grinning. Her head tips upwards to receive the sheriff's kiss.

Well, Max supposes he does know why Patty always comes back to Maplewood Grove.

"Right on time." Max smirks, gaze darting to his watch. It's barely seven o'clock. "Patty keeping you from burning that midnight oil?"

Colton slides him a sly wink most wouldn't be privy to from the stern-faced sheriff—but they've all known each other too long for formalities. It's why Max is comfortable teasing the two of them. Patty, her dark eyes sparkling with amusement, enjoys it. The sheriff, especially around his girlfriend, is far less tightly wound than he used to be.

Just as Max is about to approach, a small, excited voice cuts across the store. "Sheriff!"

All three of their attention shifts simultaneously, seeing him barrel towards them. The kid's energy is infectious. Max can't help but grin, watching him skid excitably to a sneaker-squeaking stop in front of Colton. The contrast between the kid's striped sweater and the sheriff's uniform is hilarious.

He never gets to laughing. The little straw-haired boy chatters with Colton, barely noticing him and Patty at all. But Max feels a shift in the room. It's subtle, at first. The faintest shift in energy. A quick look around confirms to Max that he's the only one who feels it. Unnerved, his eyes drift, tugged by some inexplicable force—to meet another pair across the room.

Rachel Green.

She's standing by the corner, just a bit apart from two other women—Maggie Foster, the town librarian, and Diana Hayes, the editor-in-chief of the *Maplewood Grove Gazette*. But Max doesn't focus on them. His attention lingers on Rachel, long after her warm brown eyes flicker away. Whatever magnetic pull had sparked between them still hums in the air. Max hasn't looked away by the time she looks back.

When she finally meets his gaze, Max's chest tightens. How could it not? Rachel is the kind of pretty that stirs something deep, the kind that makes you feel unsteady just looking at her. It's enough to make Max think of poetry—something he's never been drawn to. Her cheeks flush pink, and before he can react, she ducks behind the waves of her strawberry blonde hair. Her lips part—and he still sees when her breath hitches, that small, shocked halibut look on her face. An eleven etches between her brows.

His hand raises of its own accord, for a casual wave in her direction. Max can feel the tips of his ears heat. Rachel looks baffled and reluctant when she waves back. His stomach flips. His head jerks back, heart pounding in his chest. He finds Patty watching, her smile spelling *trouble*. "Not a word, Patty," Max says flatly.

And not a minute too soon, since the illustrious book club scatters only seconds after. Rachel scuttles right over, prompting Patty to cheerfully ask, "Rach. Hey, how was your day?"

Max finds he can't decide whether to be glad or concerned that Patty earns a baffled glance too. He doesn't get to a verdict. The way Rachel's shoulders slump and mouth opens... just to close again, her eyes latching to her son, steals his attention. Before Max can say anything, Patty cuts in. "Jim-Jam," she calls out to the little boy, her voice upturning in a mischievous lilt. "Why don't you show the sheriff those new books I got you for Earth Day?" A genius move Max would've never come up with on his own.

It works. Only a second later—notably, after looking to Rachel, and confirming, "Mama, can I?" and earning a kiss to the top of his head—Colton's legs are striding fast to keep up with Jamie's sprint across the bookstore.

"They let me go from the daycare place today," Rachel admits with a hefty sigh. "I'm– No. Yeah, no, I'm not doing that great." She doesn't give either of them a chance to say a thing, already adding, forcefully, "But I'll figure it out. I always do."

He can't lie; what comes out of his mouth can only *really* be described as unfortunate. Yet Max is as powerless to halt the words as he is the flutter in his belly at the sight of her. So, he blurts, "That's great!" He doesn't blame her for looking at him the way she does: like he's lost his darn marbles. He's sure she's right. "No, no—not about your job. It's their loss. But I've been needing an assistant. At the hardware store. I don't, uh... I don't wear the hours as well as I used to!" He has to ignore the choked sound to his left. Patty's attempts not to laugh are about as tactful as they are successful.

Rachel blinks at him incredulously. Still looking at him like he's lost his mind. Slowly, she says, "I don't know that I'd be the best choice, Max." Max thinks he's probably going to hell for the fireworks that go off in his head when she says his name.

He's inordinately proud of how level he keeps his voice despite it, firmly assuring, "You don't have to be." He sees her lips part again and rushes to add, convince, with an avidity he has no time to be abashed about. "It's a hardware store. Anyone good at anything has to learn it anyway, don't they? There aren't any hidden talents required for managing a hardware store. It's as low stakes as it gets. You just have to be responsible, and you are—" Max gestures vaguely, "and you are. So, what's there to mess up?"

"Well," she mutters. "When you put it like that..."

"Exactly!" Max nods eagerly. He sounds unhinged. He can't seem to stop his mouth: "Just come in on Monday! We'll dot the i's. Cross the t's." None of these phrases has ever made their way out of his mouth before. He might have to question her sanity if she didn't look as reluctant as she does.

Patty places the coffee he'd forgotten about by his elbow with a dull thump. Max's head snaps her way. Her expression says what her lips mercifully don't: *Rein it in.* She's right. He knows she is. All it takes is one glance in Rachel's direction to read the overwhelm all over her face. Her fingers twitch, fiddling with the strap of her purse. 'Overselling' is an understatement. It doesn't feel like his fault, though—like it can be helped. Something about Rachel's quiet trepidation, and the strength she clutches to like a buoy, certain she's been shipwrecked, stokes a strange fire in him. An unmanageable, inexplicable need to *fix* things for her.

"Max isn't wrong, you know," the owner of the bookstore breaks the flustered silence. The soft, pleasing cadence of her tone is the antidote to Max's harried pitch. He sees Rachel visibly relax, even if it's only by a minute fraction. And then, he tries not to be stirred up by the realization that he notices too much about her. "I think you'd be a great fit, for what it's worth. You *are* responsible. You're also funny, and clever, and great with people." Rachel's cheeks have turned the prettiest shade of rose.

"Oh, Patty, that's–" She laughs a nervous little guffaw.

"Besides," Patty continues, after pausing for the sentence Rachel doesn't finish, "like Max said. He needs help." The double entendre may be implicit, but the smirk across Patty's mouth isn't. Max's eyes roll, despite the gratitude for her quick save flaring in his chest.

Still, Rachel hesitates. Max can't miss it, the conflict raging in her eyes, shifting between Patty and him like there's a series of options she has to choose from. There's an aching desperation there, somehow. Exhaustion. Of someone who holds everything together alone, all the time—the cracks starting to show. Max remembers what that's like.

Eventually, she sighs. There's a small shift in her posture; a simple drop of her shoulders, and something hardening in her eyes. Resolve, Max hopes. "Okay," she says, not betraying a thing. "I'll give it a try. But the second I'm a burden, don't keep me on because you... You know." *Feel bad for me,* Max deduces the rest of her sentence. He nods quickly, backing off—and away, literally, with his coffee clutched in his hand.

"Great," he returns, flooded with relief he doesn't let soak the syllables. "Monday, then?"

Rachel nods. A faint smile curls her lips, but he gets the sense it's more to be polite than anything else. "Monday," she agrees. He'll take it.

He turns away, muttering a quiet "thanks" to Patty and making a break for it, before he wedges his foot any farther in his mouth.

When Max walks out into the brisk spring evening, he's still thinking about the weary look on Rachel's face. If he didn't factually know better, he would've thought her years older than she is. Rachel Green isn't the kind of girl you can forget after all, not just because she's beautiful, but because, even before, seeing her gallivanting around Maplewood Grove when she was so much younger, she'd been a light. No room could still be cold with her in it. She's different, now. Not bad, just different. Time does that, he understands it. It leaves wounds on people. With his town already growing bedecked in preparations for the Cherry Blossom Festival his late mother had been such a force behind, it's hard not to think deeply about it all. The past, the present—and all that could come.

The festival, Max can still hear his mom telling him, is about more than flowers. It's a yearly reminder that seasons pass, and change is the only inevitable thing. Renewal. Time litters people with wounds, but it heals too. Nothing, once broken, is ever the same again.

Sometimes, though, it gets better. That hope is the point.

Chapter Two

RACHEL

The lush grass brushes against Rachel's toes as she walks Jamie through the park, their hands joined in an easy swing. It feels right here—Maplewood Grove's vivid expanse on a Saturday afternoon demands it. As they walk off the mountain of pancakes from breakfast, Rachel feels a calm she hasn't known in days. The trees are still mostly bare, but there's a rich perfume of spring in the air—a breeze that smells like damp earth and fresh growth.

When Rachel was a little girl, she spent countless hours here, playing with her sisters—at least until they were too old and cool to spend their Saturdays with their younger sibling.

Most of the time, the town feels strange to her, like an echo of a life too distant to feel real. But with Jamie by her side, she stays grounded. He's the reason—the 50-something inches of pure joy—that makes her grateful for every choice she's made, as long as it led her to him.

"You think the blossoms will come out soon, mama?" Jamie asks now. His voice is hopeful.

Her hand gives his a squeeze. "Sure will, baby. Just in time for the festival."

His head tips upwards. First, to look at her, and then towards the branches that are still tangled and mostly barren—yet, here and there, began to promise small, pink blooms to the town. Rachel smiles at his wonder. She doesn't have to strain to imagine the way it will look in just a few weeks. The memory still feels like it's been plucked from yesterday: the way pale petals bathe the park in a blanket of color, scattering with every enchanting blow of the crisp air. Green dotted with pink. The way the town could look like a fairytale come to life.

"Hey, bud," Rachel tugs on his hand. "You wanna know what the cherry blossoms mean?" He has such curious eyes. Rachel remembers her own being that bright. It's a sadder 'once upon a time' than she cares to dwell on, especially when her son nods.

"The town throws a whole festival for them because they're special," she explains. "They only bloom for a short time, but when they do, it's like this place turns into an enchanted forest. They're beautiful. People say they're a symbol of new beginnings... of hope." She looks away, her voice softening, but Jamie's eyes stay fixed on her. He's a smart boy. A perceptive one. There are always more questions in his eyes than she has answers for.

She can only hope he doesn't catch it all. Not the yearning tamped into the corners of her words, or the way her heart aches in her chest. This festival, which had been enamoring but mostly meaningless amidst a slew of other festivals this town never got sick of celebrating when she'd been growing up... now means too much. All day, walking through Maplewood, Rachel has been thinking of how it was the very things these cherry blossoms represented that she needed right now. Everything, too, she's having a hard time believing in.

"I like that," Jamie says thoughtfully. "Beginnings." He sounds out the word slowly, as if pressing it into the pages of his vocabulary like a four-leaf clover tucked between the pages of a book.

His tender, untainted sweetness almost makes it possible to forget the reality of her life. *Their* lives, because he is attached to every choice she makes. She never forgets that. She's his mom; it's her job to make him feel safe, to show him everything will be okay, that life always goes on. Even when your mom marries the wrong man and gives you the wrong father and bolts towards a *fresh start* that's easier to dream about than it is to turn into a reality. Losing the job at the daycare had been far from the worst thing she'd ever been through, but it was one more thing she'd let slip through her fingers. One more sign that life isn't the stability she wants, with every inch of her heart, to give to her boy.

She can't let Jamie know. She can't let him see it in her eyes.

So, instead, she leads him to one of the larger trees. This one's branches stretch longer; its buds are more prominent, looking like berries about to burst. Jamie's eagerness skyrockets, just the way she'd wanted it to. "Will they be like this for Earth Day?" Jamie gasps, awed.

His new school project is all he talks about these days. Even through her helplessness and melancholia, Rachel marvels at Jamie's ability to tie things together, like Patty's bookstore to more knowledge, still at the age where he's ready to look things up in books instead of the Internet. And now, tying it to the town's upcoming festival, and the Earth Day activities slated to fill up the last week of April at his school. It's a warm balm to her aching heart, to see it in him. It makes her feel like, no matter how much of a failure she feels like, at least she's done something right.

"Sure will," Rachel promises. Their grip stretches when he dawdles forward to splay his soft palm against the bark. It's nothing he could've done back in the city, she knows—since it isn't the first bout of evidence that Jamie thrives here. It's why she has to keep trying to find a real foothold here.

The thought is a direct path to thinking of the evening before. Her mind just drifts. To Max Bennett, who she'd barely known growing up here, given his being a handful grades above her in school. His abrupt, immensely eager job offer. An offer Rachel doesn't even know how she feels about. Then again, it isn't like she can afford to look a gift horse in the mouth. She needs the work. Needs the money work brings in. Desperately. However she may feel about her inexperience—or how totally it intimidates her, being so far outside of her comfort zone. The daycare had been different. All Rachel has experience in is caretaking. And yet, the way Max had talked to her, so eager to help, made her want to believe in herself again.

"Come on, bud," she says, thinking about how maybe the cherry blossoms aren't the only symbol of new beginnings. "Let's keep exploring, huh? I want to show you the pond. There are baby ducks. I'm sure someone will lend us some bread to feed them."

Eagerly, it's Jamie who beams and starts pulling her along. Rachel lets him. But she keeps them carefully upright and on the right path, while he bumbles forward with gleeful abandon. They almost run right into Agnes and Mabel Carlton—a part of Maplewood Grove Rachel hasn't been tripping over her feet to introduce her son to.

The notorious busybodies always march as if in unison. Dressed in matching clothes—which, today, feature floral blouses and denim skirts—they move with more agility than one expects out of two old women in their late seventies. But it was their matching, flinty eyes that had spooked Rachel since she'd been a little girl.

"Rachel Green!" one of them (Agnes, Rachel thinks) calls out. Her voice has a piercing trill. The other one (who must be Mabel) is right behind her, her eyes glinting with mischief that makes Rachel's stomach turn. "And little Jamie!"

She's already bracing herself. There's no polite escape to be made here. They are well and truly trapped. Jamie, however, isn't afraid. He giggles, tugging on her hand. "Ma, it's the flower ladies!"

"We were *just* talking about you," Mabel purrs.

"Now here you are," Agnes adds, "like fate itself, one could say."

Rachel hears the nerves in her own stilted laughter. "Um. Good afternoon, ladies."

They nod together. Their eyes meet. "So," Mabel starts, hands clasping together in an impromptu clap. "We heard something interesting this morning, missy. Something *very* interesting." Right there, Agnes picks up the dropped thread and continues: "Sure did, sure did. We've *heard* you've found yourself a new job."

"At the hardware store," Mabel adds conspiratorially, her voice a stage whisper. Rachel sees her dentures move in her mouth.

Shock sings through her body before she realizes it shouldn't. It's Maplewood Grove. She'd lived here her entire childhood, and most of her adolescence on top of it; she knows how enthusiastically the grapevine flows. She doesn't bother fumbling. "Sure did," she agrees simply, praying they'll leave it at that.

No such luck! "A gorgeous face like yours? Oh, you'll make that place the talk of the town!" a twin chirps.

"And who'd expect such loveliness in such a... *dour* place," the other sniffs, with affected disgust. "You're doing that boy a favor."

Rachel doesn't know whether to be mortified by the compliment or laugh over them talking about a grown man nearly in his 40s like he's a teenager.

She's got no choice but to stick to the former when one twin begins nudging the other. Rachel has a bad feeling. "And speaking of Max..." a twin prompts. The other carries it forward, mouth split in a sly, unnerving grin. "Such a fine man, that one. And single. Did you know that, Rachel?"

At this point, Jamie seems to have lost all interest in this conversation. All Rachel does is drop his hand, and he runs towards the ducks – totally and completely unperturbed by the clutches he's left her in. Rachel tries to use that, excusing, "I should–" Her head tilts in Jamie's direction. Her head is spinning.

"Of course!" they allow too merrily, before undercutting it with an addition of, "But! You should join the Cherry Blossom Festival. It

119

could use someone like you. With your eye for beauty? *Tscha!* You've always had a knack for making things lovely! We remember!"

Her return to Maplewood Grove hasn't been without people making references to the girl she had been. But it's been painfully rare for it to be centered around a potential she still has. "Well, I don't know..." she finds herself saying, astonished to hear it herself. "I haven't volunteered for anything in a long time, ladies— Motherhood is..."

They never let her finish. "Exactly why we need you!" they insist in tandem.

One leans in, right in her face, until Rachel's view of Jamie is obscured by the close-up of a wrinkly, spotted face. "We won't take no for an answer, missy. You're a part of this town! Won't you be a part of the festival?"

How can she argue with that? She stumbles back a step and nods. Anxiously, her gaze slips sideways, just to catch Jamie chasing a duck. "Okay," Rachel agrees hurriedly. "Okay, I'll help out. But not today– Right now I need to go be with my son, okay?"

MAX

It's 9:08 when Rachel stumbles into the store, and everything from her hair to her face is frazzled. Before he even has a chance to say a word, she's already apologizing.

"I'm sorry, I'm sorry—am I already fired? I wouldn't blame you, I'm sorry—"

Max has to cut her off, his voice raising, "Rachel, *breathe.* You're eight minutes late. Unless you ran over my grandmother on your way here, you don't need to apologize."

That's enough to stop her short. "Isn't your grandmother...?" she asks, baffled.

Max chuckles, nodding. "Yeah. She passed away seven years ago."

That's when Max notices that Jamie's with her, clinging to her side. His wide eyes scan the store with such a confused look on his face, Max wonders if he's ever been inside one. Rachel misconstrues his glance to her son. "I'm sorry," she blurts, shoving hair out of her face that the wind outside has wrought havoc on. "My babysitter just bailed last minute, and I—"

"Rachel, you're fine," he says firmly, waving it off. It's Monday morning, and Max is certain Jamie should be in school—but it's none of his business to question. All she needs to know is, "You can bring Jamie in any time you need to."

Stunned, Rachel blinks. He can see the second relief floods her soft features. It makes his heart soar, to evoke it. "Are you sure?" she still asks. "I don't want to be a bother—"

"Why would you be?" Max returns gently. "I hired you. You're a mom. He's part of the deal. If you'd asked me before, I would've told you that anyway. This isn't an issue."

The tension seeps out of her in waves. Her shoulders are visibly looser when Max motions towards his office—or rather, the small pocket of space behind the counter that serves as one. "Just set Jamie up there, okay?" he offers. But his face, sheepish and scrunched, knows it isn't much. Neither mother nor son seem to care. Jamie pokes his head in, immediately gravitating towards the few books on his shelf. "I'll be right back," he says, stepping around Rachel to pop into the closet-sized back room, especially made up of more shelves with all sorts of odds and ends cluttering them.

Amongst them, however, is the armful of items he returns with: drawing tools, bubbles, and most prominently, a bucket of LEGO bricks. "My nieces and nephew visit in the holidays and some summers. So, I keep those handy. Go ahead, Jamie." He shakes the bucket enticingly, the bricks inside clanging noisily.

Behind Max, Rachel's breath hitches. "That's so kind," she says tenderly, sinking to her knees as he sets down the bucket. She helps Jamie pry off its top—and her eyes land on his. Warmth flares in the middle of his chest.

Once they have Jamie settled and Rachel is fully reassured she can see him no matter what angle in the store she's checking on him from, they launch into her orientation. Fortunately, there isn't much to orient to in a hardware store.

There are basics and he talks her through those. He shows her the inventory system. All of it is simple enough, but the fierce focus Rachel treats it with makes Max enjoy explaining it. Lord knows his ego, after his ridiculous behavior on Friday, needs all the help it can get.

It's hard for it to not be soothed with her following his every word, and asking pointed, purposeful questions on top of it. In no time at all, she's already grasped where to find any spare parts for certain tools should he not be available, and how to track any customer orders that come in, whether in person or on the phone.

He's pleased to discover she's a quick learner. And maybe even a great actress, since she doesn't look bored even once. She isn't frantic about checking on Jamie. Even that, she treats methodically, ducking her head inside his office in measured increments. Her attention is equally divided—and she never drops the ball. She listens like she's storing every detail away.

All of it is nothing compared to the finesse with which she handles the customer service side of it all. One exchange with one customer, and Max knows she doesn't need his mentorship. Her nerves exist—he expects them to—but she pushes past them like she's made for it, and she isn't shiny and smooth-talking; she's kind, warm, and organically charming.

In other words: She's good at this. Really good.

Watching her settle into it, guarded but poised, tugs at him like she had back in the Whispering Willow two nights ago. It's when she turns—as if that magnetism flows both ways—that Max steps back with a long, drawn-out sigh. "Looks like you're all set for now." He nods, forcing a casualness he doesn't feel. "I'll let you get to it."

He has to walk away, and he knows it. Before the warmth in her eyes can draw him any further. Max would know better even without a sizeable reminder of who's moved on to drawing in his office. Her life is full. Of stress and struggles—of a kid and a home and a brand-new job she doesn't need more complications with.

Walk away, he tells himself when he can feel her still watching. *She doesn't need more on her plate, man.*

Chapter Three

RACHEL

After a week of tireless work, she's got all Saturday off. It hadn't come without instructions. "Take it easy tomorrow, okay?" Max had said to her the day before. "You've earned it." Then he'd shot her that crooked, casual smile of his that, unfailingly, left her feeling off-kilter. Rachel has started to suspect there's more behind Max's dark eyes— the way he looks at her, almost as if he can see deeper than she's comfortable with. It unnerves her, just like the warmth that climbs up her neck every time their eyes meet, especially when it happens without her meaning to. They find each other—across the store, standing beside each other, even at the nearby diner everyone in Maplewood Grove frequents like it's their grandma's kitchen.

Rachel shakes off the thought, but the feeling of Max's presence lingers, prickling beneath her skin. She forces herself to push it away. *Today is your day to relax. Let it go.*

The air is warmer than it's been in weeks. All around town, people are buzzing with the preparations for the Cherry Blossom Festival. The last thing she needs is to think about her new boss...

with his steady, unwavering presence that somehow always manages to find its way into her thoughts.

Especially when she feels awful, dragging Jamie in tow with his backpack slung over one shoulder. A little guilt is nothing in front of town pride, though; the Carlton twins have been adamant about that all three times they'd run into Rachel that week. The day's saving grace comes in the form of Tessa, the sweet young babysitter for Jamie, who meets them near the playground. There's a bright smile on her face and a lollipop at the ready for Jamie. She says some of Rachel's favorite sentences like: "Don't worry about a thing," and then proceeds to ruffle Jamie's hair happily. "We'll be right here if you need us."

Rachel still crouches down to Jamie's height, brushing a stray lock of hair off his forehead. It's always important to her, to check in with *him* before they ever part ways for any reason. "Be good, okay? I won't be far."

"Mama, I'm always good." Jamie blows a raspberry with the typical confidence of a nine-year-old who'd woken up on the wrong side of the bed that morning. But his mood is picking up. Already, his enthusiasm is stirring, his attention drifting toward the swings and slides, and kids every which way.

Rachel plants a quick kiss on Jamie's forehead before straightening up. A small weight lifts from her chest as she watches him run off with his babysitter. She adores her time with him—his silly jokes, his wide-eyed wonder at everything—but a few hours to herself, even for volunteering, feels like an indulgence. She knows she wouldn't have any of it if he weren't able to be close by—and it leaves her grateful for Maplewood's community. Not to mention it's low, practically non-existent crime rate.

She tries to hold onto that.

Rather than signing up to be driven mad by the contents of her own brain, Rachel heads to the park to make good on the volunteer work the Carlton twins had recruited her for. She isn't sure what exactly she's walking into—for all the sweet talking that they'd inflicted on her, little actual details had been shared.

So maybe she shouldn't be as dumbstruck as she is, when fate has other plans. It's too telling, that she recognizes the back of Max Bennett's head the moment she comes across it. He's just one person amidst an entire group, all of them busy setting up booths, hanging banners, and hauling supplies.

"Well, well, well, look who's here!" one of the Carlton twins chimes in, her and her sister emerging from left field. "Perfect timing, Rachel. We need more hands for the setup. Agnes, where should we put her?" Mabel, Rachel deduces, asks.

Agnes grabs a clipboard in her spotted hand. "We've got you paired up already, missy. You'll be helping with the festival decorations, and—" The two of them grin at her with identical grins. "And guess who else is on deck?" Rachel doesn't tell them she doesn't have to. It doesn't seem like much of a win.

Rachel turns, and of course, there's Max, holding a box of banner materials. If seeing the back of Max's head had startled her, the sight of him now—sleeves rolled up, forearms dusted with sawdust—renders her completely still. And then there's that grin—the one that's impossible to ignore—spread across his face.

"Oh, Rach," he says, all mock astonishment. "I haven't seen you in *forever*."

It's so ridiculous, that Rachel can't help the laughter that she chokes on. "Oh, totally," she plays along when both of them know they've spent most of the day every day together all week.

Grinning at her, Max says, "Looks like we're on banner duty." He motions to the stack of folded banners and decorative cherry blossom streamers in the box he's holding. "We'll be hanging these around the park—trees, the main stage, that kind of thing. Shouldn't be too bad."

"Shouldn't be," she echoes. But her pulse contradictorily speeds up. It's just the way he talks to her—like they've been friends for years, and it's effortless to be her friend. Rachel knows it isn't the case. She isn't easy to be close to. His ease leaves her feeling slightly off balance, unsure how to respond to it; and yet, she can't deny she enjoys it. It's hard not to spiral around it, not helped by the fact that she's exhausted from a week of the same.

"C'mon, I'll grab the ladder. We can start by the gazebo." Max's voice pulls her back. Before she knows it, they've fallen into step with one another. Six days don't seem like they should be enough to form a habit, but it feels like one, all the same, to let him guide her. In the past week, even if only in a small, necessary way, she's come to rely on his assistance. Maybe because he's done such a bang-up job with it when it comes to the rest of her new normal.

Regardless, they fall into a rhythm they may as well have choreographed and synchronized. Hours spill away in between all the decorating. Their hands stay busy with the repetitive work of unfurling banners, securing them to posts, and adjusting the fabric until it drapes just right. For the most part, they work in comfortable silence, a quiet that never feels awkward or forced.

But it's more than once that Rachel thinks about it—about how long it's been since she worked side by side with someone. A man, no less. The thought catches her off-guard, nothing she can afford to dwell on. It doesn't seem unattached that she dives into the weaving together of intricate cherry blossom garlands. She focuses on the methodical movement of her hands.

"You've got a good eye for this," he tells her when she's sure he isn't looking anymore. "Everything looks better when you touch it." Her cheeks heat over the unexpected compliment. *It's just a comment,* she tells herself. But there's something about the way he says it—so offhand like it's the most natural thing in the world—that makes her stomach flutter.

"Years of homemaking," she offers lamely. "It's kind of my thing."

"Well, you're good at it," Max replies, so genuine. "I'm not so bad at hammering nails, but you've got me beat when it comes to making things look... inviting."

Rachel finds herself giggling. "That's high praise, coming from a hardware store owner."

He smiles back at her, looking almost proud for making her laugh. It's nice, Rachel can't help but think, to talk to an adult like this. To be seen, not just as Jamie's mom, or the woman who's been struggling to get by, but as herself.

It makes it more important than ever to keep her hands busy. When they are, she doesn't think too hard about any of it. Not his smile, or how nice his arms look, and definitely how wonderful it feels for someone to look at her like this—like she's still someone worth looking at, not just a single mom with a pile of worries.

For now, it's just this moment. This conversation.

And that's enough for her.

MAX

He notices Rachel's son lingering near the pile of wood scraps and walks up to him automatically. Max hopes he doesn't come off as creepy when he approaches Jamie, who's standing there with that inquisitive look, fiddling with a piece of sandpaper. The kid has been watching everyone work all afternoon—but there's something about him, especially the scrunched-up look of focus he's clearly inherited from Rachel, that tugs at Max's heart. He doesn't need to be told he's getting attached. He already knows.

All week, Jamie's been in and out of the hardware store. It's only natural that Max picks up on both mother and son's little quirks. Like how he's prone to sticking close to his mom, but isn't so shy that he won't scuttle over to ask Max questions about tools. Max can admit he enjoys them, the days Rachel steps out for lunch and grabs Jamie just to come back to the store. Sometimes, they bring him a sandwich—no matter how many times Max tells them they don't have to go through the trouble.

"It's no trouble," Rachel is always insisting.

Max gets it. It's no trouble for him now either as he walks over to Jamie and crouches down, just like he's seen Rachel do so many times. "It's important to me that he knows I take him seriously," she had explained when Max asked her about it a few days ago. He likes that about her. He likes her a lot.

"Hey, buddy. Whatcha looking for?" he prods playfully. Aiming for the opposite of intimidating.

Jamie glances up, biting his lip, and the action reminds him so much of Rachel's own nervous tic that Max can't decide whether he's truly unnerved or it's just a studied tic he's picked up from his mom. "I'm trying to figure out how to make something... I dunno, like a birdhouse maybe. But I'm not sure where to start."

A faint, familiar glow teems in his chest. "Well, I've done it once or twice," Max shares in a stage whisper. "How about we make one together? For one of the stands at the festival. Birds need a place to hang out, too, right?"

Jamie's face lights up, and he nods avidly. "Yeah! Yeah, sure! That'd be cool!"

Max grabs some supplies and sets them up on a nearby table. "See, this part here, we'll nail it together like this..." he explains each step as they go along, "and then for the roof, we can angle it like so. You got it? Great. Want to give it a shot?"

Not unlike Rachel at the store on her first day at work, Jamie's confidence rises palpably—by however slim a fraction. His little hands grip the hammer, the tiny pink tip of his tongue poking out in concentration as he carefully follows Max's instructions. Max watches him, fascinated. Guiding him where needed, but mostly letting Jamie figure it out on his own. The boy's gusto is infectious, and soon enough, they have a rough but sturdy little birdhouse taking shape.

When they're done, Jamie's face beams with pride. "I made a birdhouse!" he exclaims, holding it up for Max to see like he hadn't been there for every part of it. Max beams back.

"You sure did, bud," Max says, chuckling fondly. "Awesome job, dude."

Without any further ado, he watches Jamie rush off to find Rachel, bouncing all the way there. Max watches as he shows her the birdhouse, his words tumbling out in excited bursts. As always, Rachel ensures they're eye to eye so Jamie can see when her whole face lights up as she praises him. "Wow, baby, that's amazing! You did *such* a good job! I can't believe you!"

She gasses the kid up like he's just built a darn skyscraper. Jamie eats up every word, his chest puffed out with pride, the way every kid should get to. The way every dad should get to encourage their kid, Max can't help but think. To top it off, there's no staunching the pang in his chest; it's a pain like that of a broken bone, that still aches every time it rains.

Over the past few years, he's been so focused on keeping his head above water, that he'd almost forgotten. His yearning had been somehow misplaced, when there had been much bigger fish to fry. The truth is unavoidable now. Max has always wanted this—a good woman whose stories he knows, a child to share moments with, to guide, to build things together. Life hadn't gone that way for him and Julia Bennett. There were a lot of things he'd planned on his path to a rude awakening. Life, Max had learned the hard way too early on, couldn't be planned day to day and hour to hour for the years to come.

One could only make the best possible choice they could at any given moment.

Right then, Max can't help but look at the birdhouse they've put together. It renders his throat swollen with emotion. There's a lump in his throat when Jamie's little kid's laughter intertwines with the sweet spring breeze. It pairs with the deep longing settled in his bones.

He watches Rachel with her son, witnessing the way she makes Jamie feel like he can do anything—it makes him think about everything he's missed. What he still misses. He remembers. Fatherhood.

Max can't help but think again: Time leaves all kinds of wounds.

Still, helping out eases the ache in his chest, just a little. It fills some of the void that's been gnawing at him. Max can't help but wonder, even if only for a moment, what it would be like to have that kind of connection again.

Chapter Four

RACHEL

It's a slow day—the slowest one she's lucked out with since she came back to Maplewood Grove. Most of it passes in an uneventful haze. Rachel knows some people would call it boring. Frankly, she envies those people. There's nothing more glorious she can imagine... than a whole day where nothing happens.

Naively, she's daydreaming of a bubble bath and a glass of wine when she pads out of the kitchen. She should have known better than to let the calm lull her into a false sense of security. That's blown to shreds the second she hears Jamie's ragged breathing.

It's almost subtle, at first—a hint of something being off while he's bundled on the couch beside her. The stirrings of a cold, maybe. He could get bratty when he was sick, but Rachel never begrudges him that. So does she. Her mom had always said so. When she glances over, her heart crashes to a stop. Jamie's chest is rising and falling too fast, erratically. It's the sound, though—the unmistakable, pained wheeze—that jolts Rachel to her feet, her hand frantically smoothing over his forehead. "Jamie? Jamie, what's wrong?" She can't keep the panic out of her voice.

"Mama, my chest... it hurts," he chokes out. Tight and strained, he kneads a blanched little fist into his chest, like he's trying to make a hole to exhale through. Rachel's heart lurches to her throat. Her hands are shaking uncontrollably, reaching for him—grappling for a calm that no longer exists. "Jamie, baby– Baby, take a breath for me, okay? Deep breath. Like we practiced in yoga, remember? You remember that, baby?"

The bob of his head is strained. He's—he can't breathe. Not beyond shallow huffs. That strangled wheezing grows more pronounced. When he clutches at his chest, clawing at the thin cotton of his periwinkle t-shirt, his eyes are wide with fear.

Nausea hits her like a wave. Her head spins, tears springing to her eyes, but she has no time to let them fall. What's happening? Is it a heart atta—no. No, it can't be. He's only nine. He's just a boy. He can't— "Jamie," Rachel forces out, her throat flayed-feeling. "It's going to be okay, baby. Okay? I promise. We're going to be okay." Her voice tremors worse than her hands, but she can't stop. Her heart hammers in her chest, pounding like fists behind her ribs, as she dials 911.

The ambulance ride is a blur. All she knows is her hand stays holding his, squeezing it, over and over, reminding him—reminding herself—that it's going to be fine. It has to be. It will be.

His breathing, or lack thereof, just worsens. His chest palpates frantically. His inhales are no more than gasps for air; the sound so fragile, and sharp, it cuts her to the bone. Her stomach is a ruin. Bile claws its way up her throat. It's a miracle she doesn't throw up on the receptionist. She's not even sure how she manages to speak, clutching Jamie to her side as tears stream down both of their faces.

When the nurses rush him back, away, they take her heart with them. Rachel blindly stumbles after, shaking and shaking and shaking, while they attach him to machines that beep and click menacingly, putting a mask over his face that elicits a sob from the depths of her despair.

"Is he going to be okay?" she cries, and her throat is so swollen, her voice is barely audible. *He has to be. He has to be, he's her whole life.* No one answers right away. The silence is a boulder on Rachel's chest, crushing her. Time is a tightrope pulled too taut, turned fraying. There's nothing they let her do but stand there, helplessly, watching as hands fuss over her boy, terror in his eyes over strangers that crowd around him. Someone's taken a hammer to her heart.

An eternity passes before a doctor finally approaches her. "It's an asthma attack," he explains calmly, his features neutral. It's just another day for him. "Likely triggered by environmental factors. There's a lot of pollen around this time of year. We've given him some medicine to open up his airways. He's responding well."

Like the doctor kicks out her legs from under her, Rachel collapses into the nearest chair. Her shaking hands grip desperately at the arms. "Asthma?" Relief is short-lived. It's only a moment later that fear overpowers it. "He's never had asthma."

"That's not out of the norm," the doctor explains sedately. "Sometimes it doesn't show up until later in childhood. With the right care, he'll be just fine."

Rachel isn't sure her nerves will be—but she doesn't say that. Somehow, she doubts this man will care. With a flutter of his pristine lab coat, he's gone a minute later. His words still float around in her throbbing head. Her body is in motion, but mechanically so, while they shift Jamie to a bed in a corner to keep resting.

She may never rest again. The sight of her little boy's small, pale body in a hospital bed is– She can't bear it. Her hand clutches at his, his palm sweaty, but his pulse strong and steady now. His chest rises and falls in a controlled rhythm, too; it's almost like the last hour never happened. Rachel knows it did. She feels it everywhere.

Exhaustion settles around her like a cloudy haze. Maybe it's just that, the exhaustion, but her mind puts no fight up against the memory that floods her. She's been here before, after all. Not in this same hospital room, or watching the most precious thing in her life struggle to breathe—but this: being alone in a hospital room with Jamie, scared out of her mind.

She remembers it like it was yesterday, the heartbreak that dug like barbed-wire into her bruised spirit. The ever-present ache in her chest, always waiting for Jason to show up. Like he almost never did. The burdens never shared. The man she had married, who'd made vows to her, never sat beside her in better or worse. Especially not the worse.

Here she is again. *Again.*

This time, Rachel doesn't succumb to heartbreak. No, tonight she's angry.

Staring at Jamie's face, slack in sleep, and his hand limp in hers, just stokes it. Jamie's her whole world; she's his. It's always been the two of them, through everything. And it shouldn't have been. She knows it. She knows it; how doesn't Jason?

Her phone is unlocked and in her hand before she can think twice. Her thumb taps with furious jabs—navigating to the name **JASON GREEN** in her call log. He hadn't answered her last call. He'd never even deigned to call them back.

She doubts he'll answer. *Good,* she thinks. He'd only find a way to cut her off, to dodge responsibility. And Rachel has too much to say. Too much she's kept inside for far too long. Too much she's been holding back for too long. "I *knew it-*" is the first thing she spits down the line in response to the voicemail message she could recite in her sleep. "Your son could've died tonight. He could have *died,* and you're—this could be me calling to tell you, Jason, and you wouldn't even hear it firsthand. Do you *get that?* That's the kind of dad you are. The kind who can't even—"

She can't keep sitting, she realizes quickly. Her pulse thunders within her veins. Rachel gets to her feet, pacing a hot trail in a small space; a wild animal in a zoo cage, this once.

"He was so scared. He was *scared,* and he couldn't breathe, and I couldn't either. I was scared, and you- He's your son too! What's wrong with you? How can you not care? I wish I'd never married you, Jason. I wish I'd never met you. The only good thing you ever did was help create this boy. This boy, who is... Who is wonderful. He's wonderful and funny and creative and so smart, smarter than either of us, and you don't even– You don't know him. And you don't want to." Every ounce of moisture in her body must've risen to a boiling temperature. Her tears are searing trails down her cheeks. "You don't care. And one of these days, Jason, you're gonna wake up, and you're going to realize it's too late. And this little boy will be as sick of waiting on you as I was, to– to wake up. To notice him. To *love* him, like he should never have to beg you for."

Her chest aches, the pain stabbing at her. Her eyes shut, her face burying itself in her palm. "Or maybe you won't," she sighs, the wind out of her own sails. "Maybe you won't and we'll realize we're better off. Either way? You're so disappointing. I shouldn't even be shocked by it anymore." Her head shakes vehemently, pivoting harshly when she feels a pair of eyes on her, making her skin itch.

Oh, she thinks, caught like a deer in Max Bennett's headlights.

MAX

For a long moment, they just stare at each other. Max knows she's aware that he overheard every word of her pained rant into the phone, but he doesn't say anything. He couldn't, even if he wanted to, as he watches her collapse into the chair by the bed.

Max had been thinking about how he hadn't set foot in a hospital in years. The last time he had been here, he'd been with his wife. When Julia had passed... The distinct stench of antiseptic and the cacophony of rapid footsteps chased him into his restless dreams. His life had unraveled. This hospital is a reminder of it. These are simply facts. Ones, as it turns out, he's made more peace with than he'd thought. But he has. He can feel it, standing at the threshold of Jamie Green's hospital room. His attention locked singularly on the little boy who looks unbearably tiny in the hospital bed, too pale and still than he's ever seen a child.

It's even worse when they land on Rachel.

Max enters the room quietly, gently closing the door behind him. He sets two to-go coffee cups on the table by the bed before sinking to a crouch in front of her, mimicking the way he's seen her do with Jamie. He reaches for her hand—and he doesn't pause to be surprised, how easily she allows him to take it. "Hey," he murmurs softly, his thumb stroking over the ridges of her knuckles.

Her eyes are swollen and glassy, looking up at him. Rimmed with exhaustion. The cant of her head snaps the thin thread that she's been hanging by. Both her hands clutch at the swell of his arm, her face burying itself in his shoulder. Max feels it acutely, the mass of everything she carries alone in the shaky breath she exhales. "Max," Rachel heaves, "how did you even know—?"

Max lets a slight smile touch his lips. "Maplewood grapevine never fails. You know that." It isn't the win he thinks it will be, to make her laugh. What Rachel expels is a brittle sound, smothered by distress and anguish.

"You didn't have to come." She sniffles wetly.

"Of course I did," Max replies firmly. He doesn't hesitate as his hand cradles the back of her neck, fingers threading gently through her strawberry blonde hair, damp with her tears. His other hand rubs gentle, concentric circles into her back.

Eventually, she pulls back slightly to look at him. Misery creases her features, the light in her dimmed. "I don't know how this happened. Jamie– He's never had an asthma attack before. Did I do this? The festival prep... Is this my fault?" Rachel is bereft, her bundled fists quivering in his shirt.

"How could it be?" Max asks her as softly as he can muster. "You didn't know."

"It was so fast. I—I was terrified. And I'm sitting here now, totally losing it—" She falls silent when his callused thumb sweeps away her tears.

"You're a good mom, Rachel. The best mom, really. Of course, you're losing it."

"You've been through worse," she argues, raising Max's brows. "With—"

"Julia," Max finishes for her. "You can say her name, Rach. She's not Voldemort." He gives a faint smile, though it doesn't quite reach his eyes. "This place and I go way back. We brought my dad here when he had his heart attacks. And then Jules and I spent weeks in and out of these halls, praying until the end."

"Max–" Rachel sighs, and the guilt shimmering in her eyes is unnecessary.

Max shakes his head at her. "I'm okay. And my point is that this isn't a competition. Pain is pain. You're not exactly having the best night of your life in this place." That earns him a smile, albeit a feeble one.

"Was it cancer?" she asks in a small voice.

"Breast cancer," he confirms. "By the time they found it, there wasn't much to be done. She was too far along. Though we fought it until it won." His jaw tightens until he has to pry it apart, pushing back against habit to be better, as has become the philosophy of his life. "So, yeah. I know what it's like to sit in a room like this, yeah. But that's not what matters right now. What matters is Jamie. And – you. If that's okay to say."

By now, they have exchanged countless looks. Max knows it. But it's still the first time Rachel looks at him, *really* looks at him, and he can't miss something in her eyes—a gratitude and relief, that reaches out its hand to wrap around his heart. It squeezes, stirring in him a warmth long dormant.

He cajoles, "Tell me what happened?"

Like she's following suit, Rachel thumps back against the back of her chair too. "Pollen, the doctor said. Probably environmental. Maybe allergies. His chest just—got clogged up. Inflamed. He was so scared." Her voice breaks, and with it, Max's heart. But he listens. He wants to know—and he can't take it for granted, that she pours her past out like a happy hour drink. She shares, not just about this awful night, but before it, too. Everything that believing she was going to lose her son had stirred up.

About the man she'd married, right out of college. Too young to know any better—and couldn't regret, because she'd married Jason Green and had Jamie. No amount of heartache he'd caused could ever make her want to take back her son.

"Rachel..." Max murmurs, unsure what to say but wanting to offer something, anything, to take away some of her burden. In the end, words fail him. He reaches out to brush a stray lock of hair behind her ear, A touch that closes her eyes, and leaves her shoulders sagged.

He isn't sure how much time passes, with her cheek cradled in his palm, and her eyes shut. He only knows he spends it looking at her, distressed by the dark circles beneath those warm eyes of hers, and the fatigue permeating every line of her face. She sways back to lean against the wall.

Within minutes, her breathing slows, soft and rhythmic.

She's fallen asleep. He already knows he won't be waking her. But he does watch her, taking care to move back gingerly, not disrupting the static thrumming sounds of the hospital that become hazy after a while. He brushes her hair back again, and a small snore snuffles out of her in response. Despite the weight of this night, he still can't help but bite back a laugh.

He knows this is more than just a passing attraction. He feels it in every part of him, in the way his heart stirs every time she looks his way.

If he were a braver man, or maybe just a less haunted one, he would've just told her that he would drop anything for her. For Jamie. For now, settling on the floor by Jamie's bed, Max lets his mind drift, unbidden, to Julia. The last time he sat in a room like this, he was losing her. And even now, her memory lingers like a ghost, hovering at the edges of his thoughts. It's been almost nine years, but it feels like yesterday sometimes.

Time is so precious. So precious, and he feels like he's wasting it, being afraid to make Rachel's life harder. He isn't, is he? Max exhales softly, rubbing a hand over his face. There's only one person who can answer that question—and he has to let her stay asleep.

Chapter Five

RACHEL

Time passes the way that time must. In no time at all, it's a new evening.

This one is bathed in color. The Cherry Blossom Festival is finally in full swing, as the whole town has been revving for it to be. Everywhere, vibrant pink petals swirl in the breeze like a fragrant blanket. From the sidelines of sidewalks to targeted corners of Maple Grove, every which way a person turns, they can find homemade crafts, sweet treats, and enchanting flowers to keep the cherry blossoms company. Laughter tinges the atmosphere. Friends and family alike partake in games and revel in the live music that plays on in the background.

The planning may have gotten to be, but the festival itself is anything but harried. Rachel walks through it, hand-in-hand with Jamie. The buttery yellow of her soft, breezy sundress swishes around her thighs. A simple choice, but not unintentional. She knows she wore it for a certain someone. Even as she rolls her eyes at herself, Rachel can't deny the flip in her stomach at the thought of Max Bennett seeing her.

It isn't a squirming flutter of trepidation, though. She's safe with him. More than anyone she's ever known, he's proven that. He's shown up for her. Not just handsome and helpful, but kind and attentive. He'd listened—and then he'd sat watch, looking after her and the most important person in her life, when she'd fallen into a fitful slumber in an uncomfortable chair.

In the wake of it all, even more remarkable than the cherry blossoms, Rachel can feel something has blossomed between them. Something rare and wonderful. When Jamie tugs at her hand for attention, she grins back brightly. He points exuberantly at the array of game stalls, and she lets the tide of that enthusiasm take them across the Grove. Her heart is swollen—with love and gratitude. There's a skip in her step, too, about to lead him over.

A hand lands on her shoulder, sending a jolt through her. Rachel spins around, smiling, ready to tease Max and thank him for everything she's been thinking about... until the words die on her lips. Like a love letter turning to ash.

It isn't Max. Nope.

It's Jason. Her ex-husband, for all intents and purposes. Whose leonine features pose a jarring contrast against the uncomplicated joy of the festival raging around them. Jason exudes an eerie calm. Standing there, smiling down at her like... nothing is amiss. He hasn't missed a beat, as usual. Years of one-sided phone calls and lonely dinner table conversations and his side of the bed gone cold; it's like none of it ever happened.

Rachel's stomach twists into knots. Meanwhile, Jamie shrieks with joy: "Daddy!" She barely has time to process before Jason crouches down, pulling Jamie into a hug. "Buddy," he says, his voice as smooth and charming as ever. She knows that voice. She used to trust that voice more than any other in the world. It's the one that had coaxed her and convinced her everything was fine, just fine, even when it was the farthest thing from it.

She could swear her soul floats up and out of her body to watch.

It's as if from a distance that she registers Jason has stood back up, and is back in her space. It's blankly that Rachel looks at him, numb against his handsome face. If she were going to feel anything at all, she suspects it would be nauseous.

"Daddy," Jamie is whining, tugging at his pants leg. Jason's grin is confident and easy as he pries that hold off. "Are you coming to live with us again?" Now, Rachel knows she's nauseous. Jamie's question —so innocent, and young, and sweet—strikes her like a sucker-punch. Her breath catches painfully in her chest, putting a stitch in her side.

Jason chooses then to sigh, peeved. "I don't know, buddy. You'll have to ask your mama about that, won't you." It isn't a question. It's a jab. With an icicle, maybe, with the way Rachel's blood runs cold. She just—wants to run. She wants to scream and shove at him, grab her son's hand, and run as fast as she can. Instead, she is frozen. Frozen in place for Jason to eye, challenging her, without ever needing to say a word.

Feeling like a cornered animal, Rachel forces her voice to work. "Maggie, Sam..." she says, catching the attention of her friends nearby, entangled with one another against the evening chill and none the wiser about Rachel's life about to go up in potential flames. "Could you take Jamie for a bit? Please?" She can't summon self-consciousness over the way she's pleading.

Maggie, ever intuitive, picks up on Rachel's distress immediately. They aren't just book club pals; it may have started out that way, but she does have a real, true friend in the town librarian. Rachel registers, dully, that this is what it should be like with someone who cares about you. She and Sam step in, distracting Jamie with promises of more games and treats, leaving Rachel alone with Jason—and she trusts that her kid will be okay. When had she last felt that way about Jason and Jamie being alone?

Jamie is out of earshot, though. Rachel crosses her arms now, erecting the only barrier she can between them. "What are you doing here, Jason?" She forces her voice steady. But her fists bundle in the fabric of her dress, beseeching them to quit their quivering.

"I came to see my son. Is that a crime now?" Jason's words are slick, his tone disarming, but she knows him. There's always an agenda with him, always something beneath the surface.

Rachel shakes her head, disbelief rising. "You haven't seen him in months, Jason. The divorce isn't final yet, but you can't just drop in whenever it suits you."

Her voice cracks and Jason steps closer. His lipid blue eyes lock onto hers in that way that used to make her believe every promise he ever made her. "I've been thinking, Rach," he coaxes now, and she can still feel it, her heart softening in time with his tone. "About us. About... Jamie. I've made mistakes, and God knows I'm not a perfect man, but I want to make it right. We had a good thing once, didn't we?"

Like clockwork, Rachel's heart skips a beat. This is Jason, though. It's just *Jason*. He knows exactly what to say. He knows, better than anyone, how to press her buttons. "Jason..." she starts, her protest weak to her own ears.

To his too. "You know it's what Jamie wants," he persuades. "I heard your voicemail, Rach. I hear you. We could try again. For him." Her stomach is trying to claw its way up her body, intent on hurling itself out of her dry mouth. Memories flood her—of the man she once loved and the reality of who he is, both versions battling for control in her mind.

His words sink into her skin, like teeth, creeping into the cracks of her resolve. And for the first time in a long time, Rachel feels truly rattled. She barely manages to fumble out, "I'll be back, just– I'll be back," and bolts as quickly as her feet can carry her.

MAX

It isn't something he talks about very often—but he's always enjoyed this festival. It reminds him of his mom, the swirl of pink blossoms and the hum of laughter, in a way that doesn't make Max's heart hurt anymore.

But there's something else, that evening, that his eyes keep drifting toward the far side of the park. Max's heart aches as he watches the distance between Rachel and the man Jamie excitedly calls "daddy." Hearing that word—the joy Jamie attaches to it—sits like acid at the back of his throat. As if he has any right to feel this way.

He knows he doesn't. Max knows and still just watches them while his stomach tightens. He gets to spectate in real-time, the same man Rachel had been sobbing over in a hospital room days ago just waltz back into Rachel and Jamie's lives... without so much as a warning. No warning, no apologies from the look of him. It rattles Rachel, he can see that. She is shaking like a leaf in the rain. But he can't miss that she doesn't push Jason away either.

Instead, she lets him linger in her space. Looks down at him, unable to look away, when he lowers himself to talk to Jamie. She let him stand there like he had some kind of claim on her still. *Maybe he does*, he has to reason. Max runs a hand through his hair, jaw clenched. He doesn't feel reasonable—he feels anything but. And what is there to say about it? Jason Green may smooth-talk his way back into Rachel's life, into Jamie's life... and the implication alone does something to Max he isn't ready to admit.

It's too close, too personal. Not justified.

He turns away, trying to focus on the festival instead—on the laughter, the games, the smell of street food wafting through the air —something, *anything*, more his business. None of it sticks. His brain, his heart, his eyes; they all circle right back to Rachel.

The universe has a sick sense of humor, Max thinks. It isn't a moment later that she runs right into him. Frazzled, panting, her face flushed in a way that wasn't just from the spring air. The words crackle out of his mouth on their own. "Had a nice chat with your ex, huh?" The sharpness in his voice surprises even him. It hurts to see her flinch at his cold tone. Rachel blinks. "What?"

"Jason," Max emphasizes pointedly. "You two sure seemed... cozy." He regrets the words the moment they leave his mouth. But it's too late. He feels it inside of himself, the jealousy that burns a hole through his calm exterior. He sees it all over her face, too—and that's worse.

Rachel's eyes flash fiercely, her expression hardening. Her mouth purses into a flat line. "Max, that's not why I came to find you." He can hear it in her voice, how hard she is striving for patience.

Still, his arms cross over his chest, unable to let it go. "Then why? You need a sounding board before you let him back into your life? Is that what this is?"

Her face crumples in hurt almost instantly. It's only a beat behind, the swift curtain Rachel draws and masks her pain with. "I came to you because you're my *friend*," she insists. "I needed– a friend, Max."

His heart twists at the betrayal in her eyes, turning his frustration into desperation. "A real friend wouldn't let you sabotage yourself like this. You deserve better than someone who made you feel invisible. Someone who left you to raise Jamie on your own. You shouldn't have to do this alone, but you also *don't* have to settle for someone just because they're Jamie's dad. This isn't the 1950s."

Rachel's eyes narrow. He sees her throat bob as she swallows thickly. He's never heard her raise her voice before, but it does not; tenor veering more towards desperation than anger now. "You don't *get it*, Max! You don't have kids! You don't know what it's like to have someone depend on you for everything. My choice isn't just for me. It's for Jamie, too."

She'd definitely found the chink in his armor, that's for sure. She's right. He doesn't know. He doesn't know at all what it's like to have a child. And maybe that's why he's so quick to judge—so quick to think he knows better. Something for Freud to have a field day with, probably.

Slowly, he takes a step back from her. He justifies giving her the space she clearly wants, no matter how badly he just wants to take her hand. "Fine," he says hushedly, pain lacing through it. "Just let me know what I can do to support you."

Rachel's shoulders sag, her anger fading into something softer, more exhausted. Like she's a boxer and the referee just yelled time-out. The fight just leaves her body, like the bell has gone off. In its wake, they simply stand there, awkward and raw. The festival noise around them suddenly feels distant.

After a beat, Max sighs, scrubbing a hand over his face. "I'll come with you," he offers, surprising even himself. "To talk to Jason. You shouldn't have to do this alone. I won't start anything, but you don't deserve to feel outnumbered."

Rachel blinks at him, taken aback. Always so shocked. She nods, though; clearly not expecting him to still be there, still offering to help. It devastates him, that she still doesn't understand that he isn't the type to abandon someone, no matter how frustrated they are with him. Especially not someone who is Rachel Green. "Just c'mon." Max sighs wearily.

They walk together, side by side, back toward Jason and Jamie. Rachel's posture changes; infiltrated by a new kind of strength in her spine that hadn't been there before. Max knows better than to take credit for it. She holds her head higher, her shoulders squared—and Max doesn't comment on how different she already seems from when she'd first knocked into him. *Maybe his words had stung,* he reasons, *but they'd also stuck.* He hopes they do. He thinks it might kill him if she settles for this.

It doesn't look good, that Jason is with Jamie again. Father and son chat easily, and Max *can* see it—he sees how and why Rachel hesitates just for a second before stepping up to them. There is no mincing the unbridled devotion Jamie looks at his father with. Max just watches Rachel closely, noticing how she squares herself in front of her ex, more composed now.

Nevertheless, it isn't his place to interfere. Rachel had all but told him that.

Whatever choice there is to be made, it is hers to make. He has to be her friend, and her coworker, just as he'd signed up to be—and then respect her choice, whatever that choice was going to be.

Chapter Six

RACHEL

It's a later hour than she's been up in years that finds Rachel sitting at the small, round kitchen table, with a steaming cup of coffee in her hands. The soft glow of the overhead light casts gentle shadows on the worn countertops. Rachel tries to breathe evenly—in and out, slow and steady, like she's trying to calm a storm inside.

She's listening to the quiet hum of the refrigerator. The sound is a strange comfort in the stillness. Jamie is asleep upstairs, his soft breathing filling the house like a reminder of everything good in her world. She has to hold onto that. It's what gives her strength; it's the root of everything she likes most about herself.

She takes a ginger, weary sip of her coffee. The warmth settling into her chest only reminds her of how cold her bones have been all night. She can't rid herself of the tension that's been building.

Of course, that's when the source of it walks in, with his heavy, domineering gait, pounding with the impatience Rachel remembers all too well. Jason doesn't even look at her as he leans against the doorframe, arms crossed over his chest, his jaw tight. He glares right through her. "Can't sleep?" she asks softly, trying to keep the peace regardless. To maintain some semblance of calm.

But they've done this song and dance a million times by now. Already, much to her chagrin, Rachel knows he won't answer politely. The memory of their earlier argument hangs between them, like an invisible wall she's too tired to scale.

Jason is frowning. And then, Jason is scoffing. "Would've slept better in a bed," he mutters, his sarcasm as sharp as his city-boy drawl.

Rachel takes a measured sip of her coffee, the warmth doing little to thaw the chill Jason's presence brings. She'd prepared herself for this. She reminds herself of that. But somehow, his words still find their mark. "I'm not ready, Jason," she says, steady but cautious. "I'm grateful you're here for Jamie, I know he is, but—"

Jason scoffs, cutting her off before she can finish. "Just Jamie, huh? That's real nice, Rach," he sneers, his words dripping with sarcasm.

Her fingers tighten around the coffee mug. But she takes a breath —in and out, in and out, *out and through*—refusing to let him bait her. "I just need us to talk. I'm confused, and—"

Jason rolls his eyes, dismissive. "Fine, let's talk then." His tone is patronizing, like he's granting her some favor by standing here, pretending to care. Even his acquiescence taunts. It digs into her chest like a blunt blade; it doesn't break skin, but it's far from pain-less. "I never felt seen in our marriage, Jason," she shares, keeping her voice level, compassionate. *Please, see me now,* she may as well beg. "Not really. I spent so much time crying, and you... you didn't even notice. You didn't care."

It doesn't help. Jason just shakes his head, letting out an incredu-lous laugh. "You're so immature, Rachel. This isn't a fairytale. Stop quoting movies or whatever self-help crap you've been binging trying to be more interesting than your problems really are. Marriage is hard work. What did you *expect?*"

What did you expect? It's almost funny. Rachel has asked herself the same question he shoots like a dart at the bulls-eye of her heart so many times over the last few years. "No," she sighs. "Not every kind of hard is the right kind of hard." She barely finishes before Jason cuts her off again.

"Oh, come on, Rach," he mutters, waving her off like her words don't mean anything. He swats the air, like her words—her feelings, her truths—are as significant as a gnat. Something snaps inside of her, an acute breakage; maybe just the strike of a match, and then the roar of a fire igniting that she didn't even know was there. She stands up, her palms slapping flat on the table. She rises to her feet, palms flat on the table. "Stop cutting me off, Jason," her voice strong, steady, and finally unyielding. "I'm trying to talk to you, and all you do is dismiss me. I'm done with that. If you can't be a polite adult, you can go."

Jason blinks, caught off guard. Already, his mouth is opening again. But she doesn't let him interrupt again. She's not backing down this time. "I *know* the divorce was the right choice for us. You and me, we don't work. Not anymore," she says, her voice steady, gaining strength with every word. "This house isn't perfect. It's small, and I'm still figuring things out. But in the last six months, I've respected myself more than I ever did with you. I've slept better. I've laughed more than I have in years."

She pauses, looking him in the eye. "You wouldn't know that, though. Because you weren't around. No matter how many times I told you I was drowning, that I needed you... you didn't show up."

Jason's face twists into a frown, his hands curling into fists at his sides. "You can't cut me out, Rachel. He's mine." He isn't even cold. He just sounds petulant. Like Jamie, when she doesn't let him eat a cookie right before bed.

Her heart clenches at his words, for that reason—and a few others. "No," she agrees slowly, "he's ours. I know that. I'm okay with that. And I'm not trying to cut you out. You're his dad. He loves you, and I want him to keep that. I would never poison him against you or sabotage your relationship with him. But you and me... it's over, Jason. It's been over for a long time."

For a moment, the kitchen is silent.

Jason stares at her, his expression hard to read. But Rachel doesn't waver. She knows she won't. She's not going back—not this time. Not ever again. Not when she sees a future waiting, shining, like a beacon calling out her name.

MAX

Endings shouldn't take him out this badly; he has more experience with them than anything else, he thinks.

The town square is nearly empty now. The once-bustling booths, stalls, and benches have been vacated by the lively crowd. In lieu, all of it has been replaced with scattered remnants of decorations and tools. Max is balanced atop a ladder, unstringing the last string of lights from the Cherry Blossom Festival. He wipes his hands on his jeans as he climbs down the ladder, exhaustion setting in after a long day.

As he descends the ladder, he spots Rachel standing beside it, and for a second, he wonders if she's a mirage. But no—she's really there, tears glistening in her eyes. His heart stumbles in his chest, ready to leap into her waiting hands.

The sight of those tears never gets easy. It's only been a matter of hours since she'd drummed into him, how little a right he had to fuss of her. But Max knows how hard he has to rein himself in, when his first instinct is to rush to her, worry flaring up inside him. "Rachel—what's wrong?" He stops himself from reaching out, snatching back the hand already halfway to hers. No, he forces himself to hold back.

Rachel shakes her head, a soft smile on her lips as she wipes her cheeks quickly. Her eyes are on his detracted hand. She sniffles, swallowing hard. Nervously—more nervous than he'd seen her since before they'd fallen into this brisk intimacy of theirs. The *friendship* he isn't sure they still have, after their argument the night before.

"No, no, I'm okay, Max," Rachel is quick to assure. He barely has a chance to process it before she is barreling forward – full steam ahead. "I'm sorry. I hurt you last night, and I'm so, so sorry for that." Her voice cracks with earnest emotion. It's a fissure Max feels a pang in his chest; a gong striking a drum. Reverberating to his gums.

He starts to speak, but she holds up a hand to stop him. It halts him. Even before, "I need to say this," she continues, swiping fresh trails of tears that pour and pour. "I know how you feel about me. I see it every time you look at me, Max, and it scares the heck out of me. It... it overwhelms me."

She takes a deep breath, her eyes locking onto his with a vulnerability that nearly undoes him. "No one's ever looked at me like that, you know. The way you do. You're always there—always being *exactly* what I need. And I'm... I'm terrified to get used to it. Because every time I do, every time I've ever gotten close, I seem to lose what I love most."

Max's heart smarts over her words. Her words, while confessional, are too resigned. He can't bear it. He doesn't need her to surrender herself to this. He steps closer, wanting nothing more than to take away the fear and doubt in her voice—to make her feel safe, and steady, and strong. The way she does him. "Rachel," he murmurs, his hands coming up to frame her cheeks. "If it scares you, we'll take it slow. One step at a time. I just want us to move forward —together."

A hand drops from her cheek to take her hand in his, his thumb brushing lightly over her knuckles, the way it had back in the hospital nights ago. "I'm not going anywhere. We'll figure this out together. If that's what you want."

"I—" Rachel looks up at him, her lips trembling as she whispers, " I want that too. I want a home. I think you could be part of it."

It's indescribable, the joy that floods Max's heart. Leaving it so full, and yet, somehow, lighter than it has been in years. "Can I kiss you?" he asks in hoarse plea.

Slowly, shyly, Rachel nods. Her smile is wobbly—but the universe pulls the curtain on their moment, blowing a hefty, magically perfumed breeze to sweep through the square, carrying with it a flurry of cherry blossoms. The soft pink petals swirl around them, like a minor tornado to cloak their moment. Petals catch in her hair, in her eyelashes, on her lips before Max reaches up to pluck the blossom from her mouth, just to cover it with his. Her lips part in a soft gasp against his just as the unmistakable voices of the Carlton twins ring out from across the square: "Well, it's about time Max found himself a nice woman!" one of them calls, the other chiming in with a chorus of laughter.

It's the best sound he has ever tasted when Rachel's giggle spills into his mouth. The best thing he has ever felt when her hot cheek flushes with embarrassment and amusement against the reverent cradle of his arm. Max can't think a single coherent thought. He just sighs, "You're so pretty," just to have those words swept from his mouth with her sweet kiss.

The twins cheer loudly behind them, applauding sporadically in-between the chaos of their cackles ringing through the quiet square as Max pulls Rachel closer, deepening their kiss for just a moment longer. When they part, it's because they must. Because it's a worth-while sight, to watch her eyes shine with a mixture of happiness and something else—something that tells him they're on the right track.

They stand in the middle of the town square, surrounded by tools and half-finished decorations, their relationship feeling unfinished but full of promise.

Chapter Seven

IT's a slow day at the hardware store, the soft hum of the ceiling fan the only sound in the background as Max and Jamie sit at the counter playing cards. These days, slow days aren't such a rarity.

Neither is this scene: Jamie, his face scrunched in concentration, slaps down a card triumphantly. "Ha! Beat you again!" Max leans back in his chair, chuckling and pretending defeat. "You're getting too good at this, kid."

Across the room, Rachel is busy with her home improvement project, sanding down a wooden sign for the Carlton twins. They'd insisted on something special to mark their famous rose garden, and Rachel had volunteered to help as a thank-you for their meddling that nudged her and Max together. Max watches her, moving with ease now, her hair in a messy bun, paint flecks dotting her fingers. She glances up, catching his eye with a playful smile. "Hey, who was that guy checking out Izzie the other day?" she asks lightly.

Max raises an eyebrow. "Richard King. He's new to town. Bit of a mystery, actually—a millionaire or something, though I have no idea what he's doing here in Maplewood."

Rachel pauses in her work, leaning on the counter as she

considers that. "Oh, I don't know. Don't underestimate this town." She glances around the cozy store, where everything feels familiar and comforting. "It has something money can't always get you."

Max tilts his head, curious. "What does this place have that money can't buy?"

Rachel's smile softens, her gaze meeting his with a warmth that sinks deep into his chest. "Peace," she says simply. "Home."

They share a quiet moment, a wordless understanding passing between them. Max looks at her—really looks—and he knows she feels it too. No grand gestures, no drama, just the simple realization that, sometimes, time gives you exactly what you need.

One day, you wake up and realize you have everything you ever wanted.

Max reaches across the counter, his hand seeking hers with quiet confidence. When their fingers intertwine, Rachel squeezes gently—once, twice, three times—and the warmth that blooms between them feels like more than comfort. It's a quiet acknowledgment of all they've weathered, of a future just beginning to take root.

For the journey, for the struggle, for the chance to find love in the simple, ordinary moments of life.

The End

Sweet Catch

A CLEAN SMALL TOWN SPORTS ROMANCE

Chapter One

HARPER

The air in Maplewood Grove has the crisp, earthy scent of freshly mowed grass, evoking childhood summers. It's as if someone had bottled up the essence of carefree days and uncorked it the moment I arrived in town. The picturesque streets, lined with blooming dogwoods and perfectly maintained picket fences, scream *quaint* in a way that feels both endearing and vaguely unsettling to someone like me.

"Come on, Harper! The town's annual charity baseball game is a *big deal*," Patty Sullivan insists, tugging on my arm with the kind of determination that could move mountains—or at least stubborn cousins.

Patty raises an eyebrow, her smirk daring me to back out. "Come on, Harper. It's one baseball game. What's the worst that could happen?"

I hesitate, my hand brushing the edge of the oversized jersey. The words catch in my throat, tangled up in memories I've been trying to outrun.

"I'm not exactly a team player, Patty," I say, forcing a laugh to cover the unease rising in my chest.

Patty doesn't pry, but her knowing look says it all. I'm not telling her - or anyone else - that the last time I let my guard down, the rug got pulled out from under me. Relationships that felt solid turned shaky, promises that seemed permanent turned to dust. That's why I keep things light these days, flitting from place to place without getting tangled up in anyone's orbit. "It's also not *my* deal," I protest, eyeing the oversized jerseys hanging haphazardly in the back room of *The Whispering Willow,* her café-slash-bookstore. One in particular, emblazoned with "Maplewood Warriors," could double as a circus tent. "I don't exactly scream 'athlete,' Patty."

Patty tilts her head and smirks. "No, but you scream 'writer desperate for material,' and this is *golden,* Harper. Think of the blog post! 'How to Strike Out in Style: A City Girl's Guide to Small-Town Baseball.'"

"I think it'll be more of an obituary," I mutter. "Here lies Harper Lane. She came, she saw, she humiliated herself publicly."

Patty rolls her eyes with the practiced ease of someone who's had a lifetime of practice. "Oh, come on. You can't just hide behind your laptop forever. Sometimes you have to live the stories you write."

"My stories are about discovering charming hole-in-the-wall diners," I point out. "Not about getting hit in the face with a baseball."

Before she can retort, the Carlton twins—Mabel and Agnes—appear out of nowhere, armed with identical grins and enough mischief to power a small city.

"Playing in the game, are we?" Agnes chirps, her blue eyes sparkling.

"Oh, this is going to be delightful," Mabel adds, clapping her hands together. "Just keep your eye on the ball, dear. And if you can't hit it, at least try to look cute while missing."

The Carlton twins are still chuckling as Patty pulls me aside, her grin positively mischievous.

"Since you're in town," she begins, with a tone that sets off immediate warning bells, "you should help with the Pie Parade."

"The what now?"

"The Pie Parade. It's a Maplewood tradition. We bake pies and, well, parade them around town before donating them to the community center fundraiser."

"That sounds... sticky."

"It's fun! And Dot Simmons has already signed you up to walk the Lemon Meringue section."

I strolled through Maplewood Grove, precariously balancing a pie in my hands. Despite my struggle to keep it steady, I couldn't help but laugh at the townspeople's enthusiastic cheers - they acted as if I was leading the Macy's Thanksgiving Day Parade. Their infectious delight swept me up, and I couldn't help but grin. *Day 5: This town is relentless in its charm. Today, I carried a pie through the streets as if it were a prized trophy. The locals cheered like I'd just won the World Series. I should be annoyed, but I can't stop smiling.*

"You're assuming I can even hold the bat without causing bodily harm," I reply dryly, but the twins seem undeterred.

"You know," Mabel says, leaning in conspiratorially, "in '78, I was the star hitter. Scored three home runs."

"Wasn't that also the year you knocked out Leonard Beckett?" Agnes chimes in, her tone just shy of scandalized.

Mabel waves her off. "Leonard was fine. He needed a nap anyway."

Patty barely suppresses a giggle as I glance between the twins. "Is this supposed to be helping?"

"Oh, absolutely," Mabel says with a wink.

"Fantastic," I mutter, reluctantly grabbing a jersey and wondering how I ended up in a Hallmark movie.

The field at Maplewood Grove Park is a Norman Rockwell painting come to life. Rows of folding chairs form a cheerful half-circle around the diamond, while children chase each other across the sidelines, shrieking with laughter. The air is filled with the smoky-sweet scent of hot dogs and lemonade from the vendors, mingling with the fresh, grassy aroma

Day 1: Maplewood Grove smells like nostalgia, but also like trouble. The kind of trouble that comes with small-town gossip and overly friendly neighbors who bake pies. It's charming, sure, but I'm already counting the days until I'm back on the road.

Patty drags me toward the dugout, rattling off tips I'm sure won't help. "Just keep your grip loose but firm. Don't strangle the bat."

"Why does everything you're saying sound like a euphemism?"

She snorts and nudges me forward. "Just have fun, Harper. It's not the major leagues."

"That's what they'll put on my tombstone," I reply grimly.

Our team—if you can call it that—is a ragtag mix of enthusiastic locals and a few unfortunate souls like me who clearly lost a bet. Agnes Carlton is coaching from the sidelines, her floral sun hat bobbing as she shouts directions that no one seems to follow.

When it's finally my turn, I drag myself to the plate, every inch of me begging to get the heck out of there. The crowd cheers politely, the way you do for a kid trying their best in a school play.

I grip the bat, plant my feet, and squint at the pitcher, a wiry teenager who looks like he could throw the ball into another dimension.

The pitch flies toward me, a blur of white against the blue sky. I swing.

And miss.

The bat slices through the air, the metallic whoosh ringing in my ears. My heart pounds, the dry taste of nerves sharp on my tongue.

The ball smacks into the catcher's mitt with a sound that seems to echo forever. The crowd claps anyway, their applause soft and pitying, as heat rushes to my cheeks. The ball smacks into the catcher's mitt with a satisfying *thwack*.

The crowd claps anyway.

"Great form!" someone yells, and I can't tell if they're joking.

"Shake it off, Harper!" Patty shouts. "Eye on the ball!"

Taking a deep breath, I adjust my stance. The pitcher winds up again, and this time, I make contact—a dull *thud* as the ball dribbles pathetically toward first base.

"Run!" Patty yells.

"What?" I ask, momentarily frozen.

"Run!" she shouts again, her arms flailing like an air traffic controller.

So I run. Sort of. I attempt a hasty, uncoordinated dash, which inevitably ends with me stumbling and tumbling face-first into the ground.

The crowd responds with good-natured laughter, and even I can't suppress a smile as I pick myself up, trying to preserve whatever shred of dignity remains.

"Nice hustle, rookie."

The voice is deep, rich, and unmistakably amused.

I glance up to find a man leaning casually against the chain-link fence. He's tall, broad-shouldered, with dark hair curling just enough to make you wonder if he's perpetually disheveled on purpose.

"Thanks," I reply, deadpan. "It's all part of my strategy."

His smile widens, and for a moment, I forget how out of place I feel in this town.

Maybe Maplewood Grove isn't so bad after all.

Chapter Two

JAKE

The annual charity baseball game used to be my favorite event of the year. Back when I could still throw a fastball that left batters swinging at air and their pride in pieces. These days, it's just another obligation—a good cause, sure, but nothing that stirs the blood like it once did.

The truth is, this field used to be my whole world. The cheers, the crack of the bat, the rush of adrenaline as I rounded the bases—it all felt limitless. But life had other plans.

When Dad passed, someone had to take care of Mom and the farm. It wasn't even a question. Baseball dreams don't plow fields or keep a roof over your head. So I traded the big leagues for small-town coaching, convincing myself that staying here wasn't just duty—it was what I wanted.

I remember the exact moment it all changed. The crack of the bat, the sharp pain shooting through my shoulder as I stretched for the catch, and the grim expression on the team doctor's face later that night.

"You've got talent, Jake," he said, his tone heavy. "But if you push through this, you might not be able to throw at all."

At 23, I was riding the high of a minor league contract, and the choice felt impossible: gamble on a career-ending injury or give it all up. I chose the latter, trading dreams of glory for the steady life Maplewood Grove offered. Most days, I'm at peace with that choice. But on nights like this, when the field is alive, and the crowd's energy buzzes in the air, I can't help but wonder if I let go too soon.

The boys swarm the field like it's their personal playground, laughing and shouting as they warm up. One kid, Timmy, stands off to the side, clutching his glove and looking hesitant.

"Hey, Timmy," I call, waving him over. "How about you show us that arm of yours?"

Timmy grins, shy but proud, and when he finally pitches, the ball soars straight into the catcher's mitt. The other kids erupt in cheers, and Timmy beams like he just won the World Series.

Moments like this remind me why I stayed, even when the dream of playing pro faded away.

From my spot by third base, I scan the field. Kids are chasing each other along the sidelines, hot dogs and lemonade are selling like hotcakes, and the town is alive with its usual buzz. It's the kind of day that feels straight out of a postcard.

But for me? It's just another reminder of what I've lost.

"You're up, Coach," shouts Marcus, the lanky college kid we roped into umpiring this year.

"Yeah, yeah," I grumble, adjusting my cap.

Technically, I'm here to keep things running smoothly, but I can't resist stepping in to show the kids—and a few adults—a thing or two about the game. At least, that's the story I tell myself.

I'm mid-throw when I hear a shriek from the dugout. Not the kind of shriek that says someone caught a foul ball. The kind that says, *Oh, boy, here comes trouble.*

A woman in an oversized jersey is being shoved toward the plate, her arms flailing like she's bracing for impact. She stumbles onto the field, clutching a bat like it might bite her.

The sight is enough to stop me in my tracks.

"Who's the new player?" I ask Marcus, jerking my chin toward her.

"That's Harper Lane," he says. "Patty's cousin. Came in from the city. Heard she's a writer or something."

"A writer?" I repeat, watching as Harper fumbles with the bat and nearly drops it. Her dark ponytail swings behind her like a metronome set to chaos.

"Yeah," Marcus says. "Travel blog, I think. Supposed to be real good at finding, uh...hidden gems?" He shrugs. "Doesn't look like she's good at baseball, though."

I bite back a laugh as Harper takes her first swing. The bat whooshes through the air, missing the ball by a mile. The crowd claps politely, their cheers laced with amusement.

Harper mutters something under her breath, her face scrunched in frustration.

"Come on, Harper!" Patty calls from the sidelines. "Eye on the ball!"

She adjusts her stance, her brow furrowed like she's solving a math problem. The next pitch comes, and she actually makes contact this time.

The ball rolls about six feet.

"Run!" Patty yells.

To her credit, Harper runs—or tries to. She stumbles halfway to first base, her cleats catching on the dirt, and lands flat on her stomach.

The crowd erupts in laughter, and I can't help but join in. Not because I'm mocking her—she's trying, and I respect that. But because there's something undeniably endearing about the way she's handling herself.

"Nice hustle, rookie," I call, leaning on the fence.

Harper pushes herself up, brushing dirt from her knees. She glances at me, her green eyes flashing with a mixture of embarrassment and defiance.

"Thanks," she says, her tone dripping with sarcasm. "I live to impress."

I chuckle, tipping my cap. There's something about her that's hard to ignore.

After the game, I stick around to help clean up. The sun's starting to set, painting the sky in shades of orange and pink. Most of the crowd has trickled away, but a few stragglers remain, chatting and laughing as they fold up chairs and gather equipment.

Patty waves me into the kitchen, flour dusting her hair. "I need an extra pair of hands for the morning rush."

Patty tilts her head, giving me a knowing look. "And don't think for a second you can charm your way out of this. I've seen that smile work wonders, Harper, but not today."

Her teasing tone is so quintessentially Patty that I can't help but laugh. "You're ruthless."

"Only when necessary," she replies, handing me a tray of scones. "Now go before Dot starts calling me names for being late with her butter."

"I'm not much of a baker," I warn, eyeing the rows of dough.

"Good thing I'm not asking you to bake. Here." She shoves a tray of scones into my hands. "Deliver these to the regulars on the patio. And remember, Dot likes her butter on the side, not the top."

By the time the rush dies down, I'm wiping flour from my jeans and laughing with Patty about how I almost spilled coffee on Agnes Carlton. I feel a surprising warmth—a sense of belonging I didn't expect.

Harper is near the dugout, talking to Patty. She's animated, gesturing wildly as Patty nods along. Every now and then, she glances toward the field, her gaze lingering on the base paths like she's replaying her earlier misadventure.

I grab a couple of bats and head over.

"Hey," I say, interrupting their conversation.

Harper turns to me, her expression guarded. "Let me guess. You're here to offer more 'helpful' commentary?"

"Actually," I say, holding up the bats, "I'm here to see if you need a lesson."

Her eyebrows shoot up. "A lesson? On what? How to humiliate myself more efficiently?"

"Nope," I reply, leaning on one of the bats. "How to hit the ball farther than six feet."

Patty grins, patting Harper on the shoulder. "See? He's offering to help. You should take him up on it."

"Gee, thanks for the vote of confidence," Harper mutters.

"Come on," I say, nodding toward the field. "You can't get worse, right?"

She narrows her eyes at me but grabs a bat anyway.

The field is quiet now, the earlier chaos replaced by the soft hum of crickets and the occasional crack of a bat from another field. I toss a ball up and catch it a few times while Harper practices her grip.

"All right," I say, stepping behind her. "Let's see your stance."

She plants her feet and raises the bat awkwardly.

"Close," I say, moving closer. "But you'll want to loosen up a bit. Like this." I place my hands on her shoulders, adjusting her position.

Her breath hitches slightly, and for a moment, I wonder if I've overstepped. But then she squares her jaw and nods, her focus back on the ball.

"Ready?" I ask.

She nods again.

I toss the ball gently, and she swings. This time, she makes solid contact, sending the ball sailing into the outfield.

She lets out a triumphant laugh, her face lighting up like she just hit a grand slam in the World Series.

"Not bad, rookie," I say, smiling.

She glances at me, her green eyes sparkling. "Thanks, Coach."

And just like that, the day doesn't feel so routine anymore.

Chapter Three

HARPER

The post-game buzz has faded, leaving a warm, peaceful hum over Maplewood Grove. The crisp scent of freshly mowed grass still clings to the air, blending with the sweet aroma of Patty's caramel apple crumble drifting from the café kitchen. I wipe my hands on a dishtowel, watching her bustle around as she preps for tomorrow's breakfast rush.

"Not bad for your first game," she says, flashing me a grin. "You didn't even cause any permanent injuries."

I snort. "Unless you count my pride."

"Oh, please. Everyone loved you." She loads a tray of mugs into the dishwasher. "Agnes Carlton said you were the most entertaining player of the day. And trust me, Harper, when Agnes calls someone 'entertaining,' that's a high compliment."

"Glad my humiliation was so amusing," I mutter, but I can't help smiling.

Patty glances over her shoulder. "So, what'd you think of Jake?"

I freeze, the dishtowel twisting in my hands. "Jake? Who's Jake?"

"You know, the tall guy. Dark hair. Smirk that could charm the stripes off a candy cane?"

"Oh, *that* Jake." I play it cool, but my cheeks betray me, heating at the memory of his amused gaze. "He's...fine. I mean, he was nice. I guess."

Patty raises an eyebrow. "You *guess*? Harper, the man offered to help you hit the ball. That's practically a marriage proposal around here."

"Very funny," I say, tossing the towel at her.

Before she can respond, the bell over the café door jingles. We both turn, and there he is—Jake himself, leaning casually in the doorway like he owns the place.

"Evening, ladies," he says, his voice warm and just a little rough around the edges.

Patty beams. "Jake! What brings you here? Don't tell me you've suddenly developed a craving for lemon scones."

"Not tonight," he says, his eyes flicking to me. "Just thought I'd check on your newest player. Make sure she didn't retire after one game."

I cross my arms, trying to ignore the flutter in my stomach. "Retire? Please. I'm practically a pro now."

"Is that so?" He steps closer, his smirk widening. "Then how about a little batting practice?"

My eyebrows shoot up. "Now?"

"Sure. The field's empty, the weather's perfect, and I've got time."

Patty hesitates, fiddling with the edge of her apron. "You know, Harper, The Whispering Willow's not doing as well as it used to."

I pause, the lightness of our conversation vanishing. "What do you mean? The place is always packed."

"Not always," she says with a tight smile. "The big coffee chain on the highway opened last year, and a lot of our regulars have been stopping there. I've been scraping by, but I don't know how much longer I can keep it up."

The thought of this cozy café—Patty's dream—closing its doors makes my stomach twist. "What can I do?"

She shrugs. "I don't know. Maybe your blog could help drum up some business?"

Her words spark an idea, but they also add pressure. Covering The Whispering Willow could bring attention to Patty's café, but it would also cement my role as an outsider looking in. And I'm not sure I can handle that right now.

Patty pauses, her gaze softening. "You know, Harper, you remind me a lot of myself when I first opened the café. I didn't know if I could make it work, but I figured if I kept going, I'd find a way."

I raise an eyebrow. "Are you comparing my blog to your café?"

"Absolutely," she says, her tone firm. "You've got a gift for finding the heart of a place. And maybe, just maybe, you've found your heart here too."

Patty nudges me with her elbow, her grin unmistakably smug. "Go on, Harper. You could use the practice."

I glare at her, but she's already back to loading the dishwasher, humming a cheerful tune.

Jake raises an eyebrow, waiting. His confidence is maddening, but there's something about his easygoing demeanor that makes it hard to say no.

"Fine," I say, grabbing my jacket. "But if I break a window, it's on you."

The field looks different under the floodlights, the soft glow casting long shadows across the grass. It's quieter now, with only the distant chirping of crickets and the occasional rustle of leaves in the breeze.

Jake hands me a bat and steps back, folding his arms. "All right, show me your stance."

I plant my feet, grip the bat, and glance at him. "Like this?"

He tilts his head, studying me. "Close, but not quite. Mind if I...?"

Before I can answer, he steps behind me, his hands resting lightly on my shoulders. His touch is warm, firm but not overbearing, and I suddenly forget how to breathe.

"Relax," he says, his voice low. "You're too tense. Loosen your grip, shift your weight here..." His hands slide down to my elbows, guiding them gently.

"Sure," I murmur, focusing on the bat and definitely not on the way his cologne mixes with the fresh scent of the evening air.

"Better," he says, stepping back. "Now try swinging."

I take a deep breath and swing. The ball flies a solid ten feet.

"Well, that's...an improvement," I say, biting back a laugh.

Jake chuckles. "Progress, rookie. Baby steps."

We keep at it for a while, him tossing pitches and me hitting (or missing) with varying degrees of success. The more we practice, the more relaxed I feel, and the easier our banter becomes.

"So," he says, tossing another ball. "You're Patty's cousin, huh?"

I take a deep breath, gripping the bat tightly as Jake tosses another pitch. For a moment, my mind flickers back to New York—to a job I thought was permanent and a relationship I believed would last. Both were gone now, swept away in the tide of life's unpredictability.

Staying put and letting roots grow feels like tempting fate. You get comfortable, and then the ground shifts. That's why I keep moving, keep searching for something new. But here, with Jake's steady gaze and Maplewood Grove's quiet charm, I feel the first cracks in that armor. And it terrifies me.

"That's right," I reply, swinging and missing. "She roped me into this game as part of my 'small-town experience.'"

"Does that include face-planting in the dirt?"

"Apparently." I shoot him a look, and he grins.

After a particularly solid hit, I lean on the bat, catching my breath. "What about you? What's your story, Coach?"

"Not much to tell," he says, shrugging. "Grew up here, played a little ball, came back to coach when my playing days were over."

"Not much to tell?" I repeat, raising an eyebrow. "I doubt that."

He shrugs again, but there's a flicker of something in his eyes—something that tells me there's more to his story than he's letting on.

Before I can press further, he tosses another ball, and I focus on the swing. This time, it soars past the infield, bouncing against the chain-link fence.

"Not bad, rookie," Jake says, tipping his cap.

I glance at him, and for the first time, I feel a spark of something I can't quite name.

Maybe this small-town adventure won't be so bad after all.

Chapter Four

JAKE

Maplewood Grove has a rhythm, a steady beat that lulls you into thinking nothing ever changes. Most days, I find that comforting, like a favorite song playing on repeat. But tonight, it's grating, the quiet amplified by the thoughts ricocheting in my head.

I didn't mean to overhear Harper's conversation with Patty. I was just grabbing my jacket from the café's coat rack when her voice carried over.

"This town is adorable," she'd said, her tone light but unmistakably sarcastic. "It's like stepping into a Hallmark movie. Honestly, I could write a whole post on small-town quirks. You've got Dot with her endless trivia, the Carlton twins with their synchronized banter—it's pure gold."

Patty laughed. "That's Maplewood Grove for you. But you've got to admit, there's a certain charm to it."

"Oh, for sure," Harper replied. "It's cute in a 'visit and then leave' kind of way. I mean, I can't imagine actually living here."

Her words sting more than I care to admit. Maybe it's because I've spent years convincing myself that staying here was enough, that

Maplewood Grove could be more than just a backdrop to someone else's life.

When I was younger, people told me I could make it big. My fastball had scouts taking notice as batters swung at nothing but air. But life here moves in its own rhythm, and I let myself get caught in it—staying for family, for friends, for a life that's steady and predictable.

Hearing her talk about this place like it's disposable, like it's just a stop on her way to somewhere better, reminds me of what I gave up. And it hurts more than it should.

That's when I walked out the door.

I'm not sure why her words hit me the way they did. She's a city girl, a travel blogger—it's not like she ever claimed to want a slice of small-town life. But hearing her talk about Maplewood Grove like it's a novelty to be mined for content...

I shouldn't care.

But I do.

The next day, I'm at the high school, setting up for practice. The boys filter onto the field one by one, their laughter filling the air as they toss balls and loosen up. Normally, this is my favorite part of the day. But not today.

Marcus catches up to me, holding an envelope. "Hey Coach, this came for you."

I take it, frowning as I recognize the return address—a college athletics program I'd applied to on a whim years ago. "Thanks," I mutter, stuffing it into my bag.

Later, I sit in the dugout, staring at the letter. Inside is an offer—an assistant coaching position at a Division II school in another state. It's more than I ever thought I'd get after leaving baseball behind, and it's everything I thought I wanted.

But the idea of leaving Maplewood Grove, of leaving the kids I've been coaching and the life I've built here, doesn't feel as simple as it should. And then there's Harper—complicated, frustrating, fascinating Harper.

Marcus asks, "You okay? You look...off." I tuck the letter back into the envelope, my chest tightening with indecision.

"I'm fine," I say, maybe too quickly.

He raises an eyebrow but doesn't push.

"Let's start with some fielding drills," I say, clapping my hands. "Line up!"

The boys scatter into position, and the familiar rhythm of the game takes over. I focus on the mechanics—foot placement, timing, follow-through—but Harper's words replaying like a bad highlight reel.

When practice ends, I hang back, letting the boys head home. The sun dips lower in the sky, casting long shadows across the field. I grab a bucket of balls and start pitching to the empty plate, the motion is automatic, almost meditative.

I don't hear her approach.

"Working on your curveball, Coach?"

I glance up to see Harper standing by the fence, her hands tucked into the pockets of her jacket. She's smiling, but there's a flicker of uncertainty in her eyes.

"Just burning off steam," I say, straightening.

She tilts her head. "Something on your mind?"

"Not really," I reply, but my tone betrays me.

She doesn't push, just steps closer and picks up a stray ball. "Mind if I try?"

I hand her the bat without a word and step back, watching as she takes a few practice swings.

"Ready?" I ask.

"Ready," she says, but her stance is all wrong.

I pitch anyway, and the ball sails past her untouched.

"Wow," she mutters, adjusting her grip. "Maybe I should stick to writing."

"Writing about how quirky small towns are?" I say, the words slipping out before I can stop them.

She freezes, lowering the bat. "What's that supposed to mean?"

I sigh, raking a hand through my hair. "Look, Harper, I know this is just a pit stop for you. You're here for the stories, the material. That's fine. But for some of us, this isn't a novelty. It's home."

Her eyes narrow, her expression hardening. "I never said it wasn't."

"You didn't have to," I say, my voice sharper than I intended. "I heard you last night. Talking to Patty about how you couldn't imagine living here, how this place is 'cute' in a temporary kind of way."

Her cheeks flush, whether from anger or embarrassment, I can't tell. "That's not what I meant," she says quietly.

"Then what did you mean?"

She doesn't answer right away, gripping the bat so tightly her knuckles turn white. When she finally speaks, her voice is measured. "I'm not trying to disrespect your town, Jake. I like it here. I just... don't know if I belong."

My eyes narrow, my easygoing demeanor hardening. "You keep saying you don't belong, Harper, but maybe that's just an excuse. Maybe you're too scared to try."

Her mouth falls open, and for a moment, she's speechless. "Scared? Of what?"

"Of staying somewhere long enough for it to matter," I snap. "You breeze into town, write about how charming it all is, and then move on before anyone can ask you to care."

"That's not fair," she fires back, her voice rising. "You don't know anything about why I left the city or what I've been through."

"Then tell me!" I say, stepping closer, my voice almost pleading. "Tell me why you're so determined to keep everyone at arm's length."

She shakes her head, her throat tightening. "You wouldn't understand."

"Try me," I challenge, but when she doesn't respond, I exhale sharply, my frustration palpable. "You know what? Maybe I don't want to understand. Maybe I'm done trying to get through to someone who won't let me in."

"Thanks for the practice," she says, her tone clipped. "See you around, Coach."

I watch her walk away, the ache in my chest growing heavier. The letter from the college is still in my bag, its weight a constant reminder of the choice I have to make.

Part of me wants to run after her, to tell her that staying here—staying with her—feels like the first real thing I've had in years. But what if she's right? What if Maplewood Grove is just a stop on her way to something bigger?

And what if this coaching offer is my only chance to make something of myself again?

I let her go, my heart pounding with the realization that no matter what I choose, something—or someone—I care about will slip through my fingers.

Chapter Five

HARPER

The crowd at Maplewood Grove Park is rowdier than I anticipated, their cheers and laughter blending into an enthusiastic small-
town roar. The final inning is underway, and everyone is on their feet,
rallying behind their teams with an intensity that borders on absurd.

And I'm about to make a complete fool of myself.

"Harper, you don't *have* to do this," Patty whispers, her hand
squeezing my arm. "Nobody will think less of you if you sit this one
out."

She's lying. I can see it in her eyes, the way her lips twitch like
she's holding back a laugh.

"I'm already in the jersey," I say, forcing a grin. "Might as well go
down swinging."

"Atta girl." She pats my shoulder, but I catch her exchanging a
knowing look with Mabel Carlton, who's sitting on the bench with
her knitting.

The announcer's voice booms through the crackling speakers.
"And stepping up to the plate, we have... Harper Lane!"

The crowd claps and cheers, though I swear I hear a few chuckles mixed in. Taking a deep breath, I grab the bat and head toward the plate, my heart pounding like a drum.

The pitcher looks more confident than anyone has a right to be, and the ball in his hand might as well be a meteor hurtling toward Earth.

"Don't overthink it!" someone shouts from the crowd.

Easy for them to say. They're not the ones about to embarrass themselves in front of half the town.

I adjust my grip on the bat, trying to remember Jake's advice from our impromptu practice session. Relax your shoulders. Loosen your grip. Eye on the ball.

"Need a pep talk?"

I glance over my shoulder and find Jake standing near the dugout, his arms crossed and a faint smile playing on his lips.

"I thought coaches stayed on their side of the field," I tease, though my voice wavers slightly.

"Not when a rookie's about to hit a home run," he replies, stepping closer.

A laugh escapes me, more nervous than anything. "That's optimistic."

"Not really," he says, his tone softer now. "You've got this, Harper. Just breathe, focus, and don't let the pressure get to you."

His confidence is maddeningly steady, like he actually believes I can do this. And somehow, that belief seeps into me, warming me from the inside out.

I nod, gripping the bat a little tighter. "Okay. Breathing. Focusing. Not panicking."

"Good." He steps back, tipping his cap. "Now show them what you've got."

The pitcher winds up, his arm slicing through the air like a scythe. The ball hurtles toward me, a blur of white against the blue sky.

I swing.

The crack of the bat meeting the ball echoes across the field, sharp and satisfying. For a moment, I just stand there, stunned, as the ball soars over the infield.

"Run, Harper!" Patty shouts, her voice high and frantic.

My legs finally kick into gear, and I sprint toward first base, the cheers of the crowd ringing in my ears. The ball bounces in the outfield, and I hear someone yell, "Go for two!"

I push harder, my lungs burning as I round first and head for second. When I finally slide into the base, the dust settles around me, and the umpire's call rings out: "Safe!"

The crowd erupts, clapping and cheering, and for the first time since I arrived in Maplewood Grove, I feel like I belong.

Back at the dugout, I collapse onto the bench, my heart racing and my face flushed. Jake appears moments later, handing me a bottle of water.

"Nice work," he says, his smile wide and genuine.

"Thanks," I reply, still catching my breath. "I couldn't have done it without your pep talk."

He leans against the fence, his expression softening. "You didn't need my help, Harper. You had it in you the whole time."

I glance at him, the weight of his words settling over me like a warm blanket. For the first time, I realize that maybe I don't have to keep running from place to place, looking for something I can't define. Maybe what I've been searching for is already here.

"Jake," I begin, but the announcer's voice cuts me off, calling the next batter. He tips his cap again and steps back, his gaze lingering on me for just a moment longer than necessary.

As I watch him walk away, a smile tugs at my lips. Maybe Maplewood Grove is exactly what I needed, after all.

Chapter Six

JAKE

The charity auction is the town's last hurrah for the day, and the community center is buzzing with energy. Rows of tables covered in checkered cloths line the room, piled high with homemade pies, knitted scarves, and hand-painted signs that read "Home Sweet Home" – Maplewood Grove at its warmest, most vibrant, and slightly quirky best.

I glance around, nodding at familiar faces and forcing smiles where necessary. Normally, I enjoy these events, but tonight, my mind is elsewhere—specifically on Harper.

She's standing by the dessert table, chatting with Patty and looking like she belongs here. That thought unsettles me more than I'd like to admit. After our game earlier, something shifted. Seeing her determination, her willingness to laugh at herself—it's like she peeled back a layer, and now I can't stop thinking about what's underneath.

"You gonna make your move, Coach?" Marcus's voice cuts through my thoughts.

Marcus smirks, his lanky frame leaning against the wall. "Man, the whole town's betting on you two, you know. It's like the Maple-wood version of the Bachelor."

Jake groans. "Do you ever take anything seriously?"

"Sure," Marcus says with mock solemnity. "Like Dot's trivia nights. But come on, Coach, don't make me write a love letter for you."

I blink, realizing he's standing beside me with a knowing grin.

"Don't you have better things to do?" I ask, rolling my eyes.

"Not really," he says, leaning against the wall. "Come on, Jake. It's obvious you're interested. Everyone sees it."

I glance at Harper again, my stomach twisting. "She's not staying."

"Maybe she will," Marcus says, shrugging. "But you'll never know if you don't try."

The auction kicks off with Dot Simmons at the podium, her voice carrying over the crowd like a seasoned pro. Item after item is sold, the bids flying fast and furious.

"Up next," Dot announces, "we have something very special: a picnic basket prepared by none other than Patty Sullivan!"

The crowd claps and cheers as Patty waves from her spot beside Harper.

"And," Dot adds, her eyes twinkling, "the winning bidder gets to share this lovely meal with Patty's charming cousin, Harper Lane."

My head snaps up, my pulse quickening. Harper's eyes widen, and she turns to Patty with a look that could melt steel.

"Oh, don't give me that look," Patty says, grinning. "It's for charity."

Dot starts the bidding, and hands shoot up immediately.

"Twenty dollars!"

"Thirty!"

"Forty!"

The numbers climb steadily, the room buzzing with excitement. Harper looks mortified, her cheeks flushed, but there's a flicker of amusement in her eyes too.

"Seventy!"

"Eighty!"

Before I know it, my hand is in the air. "One hundred!"

The room falls silent for a beat, all eyes turning to me. Dot's smile widens, and I swear I see Patty smirk.

"One hundred from Jake Weston!" Dot calls. "Do I hear one twenty?"

The room stays quiet.

"Going once, going twice... Sold to Jake Weston!"

The crowd erupts in applause as Dot bangs the gavel. Harper looks at me, her expression a mix of surprise and something softer, something I can't quite place.

We step outside into the crisp night air, the picnic basket in hand. The sky is blanketed with stars, a sprawling canvas of light. The night air carries the faint sweetness of blooming wildflowers and the tang of freshly cut grass. A soft breeze ruffles the edge of the blanket, and the distant hum of crickets fills the quiet. Jake leans closer, his cologne—a warm, woodsy scent—mixing with the earthy aroma of the park. The weight of his hand on mine is grounding, a quiet reassurance that feels as natural as the stars above us.

"Did you really just spend a hundred dollars on a picnic?" Harper asks, her voice teasing but her gaze warm.

"It's for a good cause," I reply, shrugging. "And maybe I wanted to spend a little more time with you."

She looks at me for a long moment, her green eyes searching mine. "You're full of surprises, Coach."

"Stick around," I say, smiling. "You might find a few more."

We settle on a patch of grass near the edge of the park, the basket between us. Harper unpacks the food—sandwiches, fruit, and a thermos of iced tea—while I spread out a blanket.

"This is nice," she says, her voice softer now.

"Yeah," I reply, watching her. "It is."

The conversation flows easily, our laughter mingling with the rustle of the trees. We talk about everything and nothing—her blog, my coaching, the quirks of Maplewood Grove.

At one point, she looks up at the stars, her expression thoughtful. "I didn't mean what I said to Patty, you know. About this place being a 'visit and leave' kind of town."

I glance at her, my chest tightening. "What did you mean, then?"

She hesitates, fiddling with the corner of the blanket. "I've spent so much time running from place to place, looking for something I couldn't even define. But here..." She pauses, her gaze meeting mine. "Here feels different."

The words hang between us, fragile and full of promise.

"Harper," I start, but she leans closer, her hand brushing against mine.

"Jake," she says softly, her voice barely a whisper.

The distance between us vanishes in an instant. Her soft lips meet mine, tentative at first but soon growing more passionate. It's like the world fades away, leaving only the two of us under the stars.

When we finally pull back, her cheeks are flushed, her eyes bright.

"Maybe this is what I've been searching for," she says, her voice trembling slightly.

I take her hand in mine, my thumb brushing over her knuckles. "Maybe it's what I've been waiting for too."

For the first time in years, I feel like I'm exactly where I'm supposed to be.

Chapter Seven

HARPER

The stars above Maplewood Grove seem impossibly bright, a glittering canopy that stretches across the velvety darkness. It feels so peaceful out on the edge of the park, where Jake and I have settled on the blanket from the picnic basket he bought.

"Not bad for a charity auction," I say, taking another bite of the apple slice in my hand. "You got your money's worth."

Jake smirks, leaning back on his elbows. "If you're the prize, I'd say it was a steal."

His words send a shiver through me, the kind that's equal parts exhilaration and vulnerability. I look at him, his dark eyes reflecting the starlight, and wonder how this small-town baseball coach managed to upend the careful, cynical shell I've built around myself.

"So," he says, breaking the silence, "what happens next?"

I frown, pretending to think it over. "Well, I write a blog post about the most charming hole-in-the-wall town I've ever visited, then move on to the next stop."

Jake's smile falters, and I realize too late that my sarcasm might have hit a little too close to the truth.

"Jake—"

"I get it," he says, sitting up. His voice is steady, but there's a tightness in his jaw that wasn't there a moment ago. "You're not staying. That's okay. Maplewood Grove isn't for everyone."

The ache in his words surprises me. I reach for his hand before he can pull away, my fingers curling around his.

"That's not what I meant," I say softly. "I don't know what happens next. For the first time in a long time, I don't have a plan. But…" I hesitate, the vulnerability clawing at my throat. "But I like it here. I like this place. I like you."

The words hang in the air as Jake studies me, his steady gaze as infuriating as it is comforting. He doesn't push, but I can tell he's waiting—hoping—for something more.

Later that night, I paced the worn wooden floor of the cozy guest room at Patty's. Staying here, in this quiet town, feels like giving up on the part of me that's always searching, always moving. I sit on the edge of the bed, my thoughts wandering back to the day it all started. The glossy office, the sharp scent of freshly brewed coffee, and the HR rep's carefully worded dismissal.

"We're downsizing," she'd said, her smile thin and apologetic. "It's not personal, Harper."

It felt personal. Losing that job, the one I'd worked so hard for, had unraveled everything. My relationship crumbled soon after—my ex couldn't handle my sudden spiral. So I packed up my life, trading permanence for the open road, promising myself I'd never stay in one place long enough to risk losing everything again.

Now, sitting here in Maplewood Grove, the thought of staying—of risking—scares me as much as leaving used to.

But leaving feels… wrong. The thought of saying goodbye to Jake twists something deep in my chest, something I've tried to keep locked away.

I glance at my laptop, where an unfinished draft of my latest blog post waits. The title blinks at me: *Finding Home in the Unexpected.*

For the first time, I wonder if I've been running from the idea of home all along.

Jake's gaze softens, his fingers tightening around mine. "You're not just saying that because I spent a hundred bucks on a picnic, are you?"

I laugh, the sound breaking the tension between us. "You caught me. I'm a sucker for a man with a picnic basket."

His smirk returns, but there's something deeper in his eyes now, something warm and unwavering. "You know, Harper, you don't have to figure it all out right now. Stay a while. See where it goes."

The idea sends a thrill through me, though it's tinged with fear. I've spent so much time running—running toward adventure, away from commitment, searching for something I couldn't name. But here, with Jake, the ground feels solid for the first time.

The next morning, I take a walk through Maplewood Grove, letting the town's quiet charm wrap around me. Dot Simmons waves from her porch, a half-finished quilt spread across her lap. At the café, Patty is wiping down tables, humming a tune I've come to recognize as her go-to when she's content. Even the Carlton twins are out, arguing over which flowers to plant in the town square.

It's not just the people, though—they're wonderful, quirky, and endearing in their own way. It's the way this place feels like a patch-work quilt, stitched together with love and imperfection. I've always thought of small towns as places to visit, not stay. But this one has a way of making you linger.

By the time I reach the park, where the morning sunlight filters through the trees, I feel lighter. Staying here isn't just about Jake. It's about finding a place that feels like home.

"I think I'd like that," I say, the words tentative but honest.

Jake leans closer, his hand brushing a stray strand of hair from my face. "Good. Because I think I'd like it too."

Jake

The next morning, the buzz of the town feels lighter, like the entire community is riding the high of the charity game and auction. I can't stop thinking about Harper, about the way her laughter carried through the night, about the way she looked at me like I was more than just some washed-up ballplayer turned coach.

As I walk through town, people wave and nod, their smiles knowing. Maplewood Grove isn't a place where you can hide your business for long.

"Morning, Coach!" Marcus calls from the hardware store. "Heard you cleaned up at the auction last night."

"Something like that," I reply, shaking my head.

"Guess that rookie you've been training is sticking around for a bit, huh?"

I glance toward *The Whispering Willow,* where Harper's silhouette is visible through the window. She's helping Patty rearrange the book display, her laughter spilling out onto the street.

"Yeah," I say, a slow smile spreading across my face. "I think she might be."

I linger outside The Whispering Willow, watching Harper through the window. She's folding books into a display, her movements graceful and easy, like she's always been a part of this place. My chest tightens.

That envelope is still sitting on my kitchen table, unopened since the night I read it. I don't need to read it again to know what it says. It's a chance—a good one—but it doesn't feel right. Not anymore.

I step inside and grab it, folding the letter neatly before tossing it into the trash. A part of me aches at the finality of it, but another part feels lighter.

I don't need to chase something I already have.

What if she doesn't stay? The thought is a sucker punch, leaving me breathless. For years, I told myself I was fine alone. But Harper's changed that. She's changed me.

As the door jingles open and she steps out, our eyes meet, and I know I have to tell her how I feel before it's too late.

Marcus grins. "Good for you, man. She seems like a keeper."

I nod, my chest tightening with something that feels a lot like hope.

Harper

A week later, I'm sitting on the porch of Patty's café, my laptop open and a steaming cup of coffee in hand. The morning sunlight filters through the trees, casting dappled patterns on the wooden planks. From my spot, I can see Dot Simmons setting up her trivia board outside the general store and the Carlton twins debating flower arrangements near the square. The town feels alive in a way I never expected to notice—or appreciate.

The email came late last night, the notification lighting up my phone with a ping. I didn't open it right away. Now, I glance at the subject line again—*Freelance Opportunity: Monthly Column on Travel and Lifestyle*—and my heart skips a beat.

It's a major publication, one I've dreamed of working with for years. The job would require constant travel, hitting the road again, leaving everything behind—including Maplewood Grove. Including Jake.

I sip my coffee, but the bitterness on my tongue has nothing to do with the brew. My laptop screen stares back at me, the cursor blinking under the draft of a blog post I've been struggling to write.

Day 1: Maplewood Grove smells like nostalgia, but also like trouble. The kind of trouble that comes with small-town gossip and overly friendly neighbors who bake pies. It's charming, sure, but I'm already counting the days until I'm back on the road.

I shake my head, scrolling to my next entry.

Day 7: There's something infuriatingly endearing about this place.

The people, the traditions, the way they cheer for someone as hopeless as me on the baseball field. I hate to admit it, but I'm starting to feel like I belong.

A soft breeze ruffles the pages of my notebook beside me, and I glance toward the baseball field in the distance. Memories of Jake's patience during our practice sessions, his easy smile, and the way he looked at me during the auction flood my thoughts.

The decision should be simple—this job is everything I've been working toward. But the weight of it feels suffocating, like choosing it would mean closing the door on something I didn't even know I wanted until now.

Jake finds me on the porch, his familiar silhouette leaning against the railing. "Stuck?"

His voice pulls me from my thoughts. I look up, startled but grateful. "Something like that," I admit, gesturing toward the screen.

He steps closer, peering over my shoulder. "You could always just write, 'Maplewood Grove: Come for the baseball, stay for the guy who taught you how to hit.'"

A laugh escapes me, breaking the tension. "Tempting, but I think I'll go with something a little less obvious."

Jake sits beside me, his hand finding mine. "Whatever you write, I'm glad you're here, Harper."

I squeeze his hand, my chest tightening. "Me too."

After Jake leaves, I wander through the town. The streets are quiet now, the early bustle giving way to the peaceful hum of a sleepy afternoon. As I stroll, I pass by familiar sights - Patty rearranging books with her signature precision at The Whispering Willow, Dot quizzing a group of teenagers on state capitals, and the Carlton twins offering a cheerful nod.

This place isn't just charming or quirky—it's woven itself into me in ways I didn't expect. It feels like a patchwork quilt, stitched together with care. And maybe I'm ready to be part of it.

When I return to my laptop, the words flow easily:

Day 14: Maplewood Grove isn't just a town; it's a story. A story about second chances, quiet bravery, and finding a home in the most unexpected places.

For the first time, I'm not just writing about a place. I'm writing about home.

The End

Sweet Melody

A CLEAN SMALL TOWN YOUNG LOVE
ROMANCE

Chapter One

JASMINE

The Folk Music Festival is the biggest event of the year in Maplewood Grove. It's the one time the sleepy town wakes up and hums with life, with musicians, artists, and vendors flooding the streets. There's this sense of electricity in the air, like something magical could happen at any moment.

And for the first time, I'm a part of it. Not just as a spectator, but as a performer.

I take a deep breath as I adjust the camera strap slung over my shoulder. The familiar weight of it steadies me, like a talisman, as I step into the bustling crowd. I'm not just here to play music; I'm also photographing the event for the Whispering Willow's social media. Mr. Stevens, the owner of the bookstore-slash-café, put me in charge of their online presence, and it's a good gig. Plus, it gives me an excuse to sneak around the festival, capturing the energy of the crowd before I have to get on stage myself.

I stop in front of the festival's main stage, snapping a shot of the bluegrass band currently performing. The music is raw and soulful, with the twang of the banjo and the deep hum of the double bass filling the air. My heart skips a beat—this is the kind of sound I love. It's gritty, heartfelt, and it feels like home, even though my roots are far from Appalachian.

The thought makes me pause. I'm Chinese-American, but I've always felt disconnected from that part of myself. My parents are super traditional, and I grew up in a house filled with Mandarin and cultural expectations. But me? I'm about as Americanized as you can get. Still, lately, I've been exploring that side of myself more—trying to find ways to blend my heritage with my passions. Maybe that's why I'm drawn to photography. It lets me capture stories, moments, and fragments of identity that I'm still figuring out.

As I take another picture, the band's music pulses through the ground, making my foot tap along. Music has always been the one thing that makes me feel truly free, even when everything else in my life feels uncertain.

"You ready for your set later?" asks Rosa, my best friend, nudging me with her elbow as she appears out of nowhere.

I grin. "As ready as I'll ever be."

"Jasmine Turner, professional photographer and future blue-grass superstar," Rosa teases, twirling one of her long braids.

"Hardly," I say with a laugh, though my stomach does flip a little. I'm excited and nervous all at once.

"Come on, you'll be great. And who knows? Maybe there'll be a cute guy in the audience, cheering you on."

I roll my eyes but can't stop the blush that creeps up my neck. "Rosa, stop."

"I'm just saying!" she says with a grin before running off to catch the next act.

I glance back at the stage, my thoughts racing. I've been so focused on what comes next—whether it's college, photography, or music—that I haven't let myself think about other things. Like love. Or even just a little romance.

I take another breath and adjust my camera. Maybe this summer is about more than just finding my footing with music and photography. Maybe it's about figuring out who I am and what I want.

Eli

The festival is buzzing, but it feels like I'm floating through it. The music, the crowd—it's all background noise. Not in a bad way, though. More like a melody that's always playing underneath everything. I'm not here for the noise. I'm here for the quiet moments in between. That's where I find my words.

I glance down at the small notebook in my hand, flipping through the pages. I've been scribbling down bits of poems all day—pieces of phrases that drift through my mind like lyrics waiting to be sung. Poetry's always been my thing, ever since I was a kid. I guess that's why I feel so drawn to the Folk Music Festival. There's a connection between poetry and music, a rhythm to both that makes me feel... at home.

As I wander through the crowd, I catch snippets of the performances—bluegrass bands, acoustic sets, and even a lone fiddler playing on a street corner. The sounds blend together into something bigger, something alive. But there's one sound that pulls me in more than the others.

A girl's laugh.

I turn my head, my gaze landing on a girl with a camera, her face lit up as she talks to her friend. She's not just laughing—she's alive. Her energy crackles in the air, making her stand out from the crowd like she's the one who's supposed to be on stage, not in it.

I pause, my heart beating faster than I'd like to admit. She's got this look about her—confident, sure of herself—but there's something in the way she holds her camera, the way she watches the stage with a thoughtful expression, that makes me think there's more to her than what you see on the surface.

I tuck my notebook into my back pocket and take a step closer, careful not to get too close. I don't know why I'm so curious about her, but I am. Maybe it's because she's different. Or maybe it's because I've been spending too much time inside my own head, wrapped up in poetry and books, and not enough time in the real world.

Before I can stop myself, I hear my own voice. "You into photography?"

She looks up, surprised, her eyes locking onto mine. They're dark, with a glint of curiosity that matches my own. "Yeah," she says, adjusting the camera strap on her shoulder. "I run the social media for Whispering Willow bookstore."

"Cool," I say, shoving my hands into my pockets. "I spend a lot of time in that bookstore."

Her eyes brighten with recognition. "Wait, I think I've seen you there. You're the guy who's always reading poetry, right?"

I feel a flush creep up my neck. "Uh, yeah. I guess that's me."

She smiles, and for a second, I forget that we're strangers standing in the middle of a crowded festival. It feels... easy. Like talking to her is something I've done a hundred times before.

"I'm Jasmine, by the way," she says, extending her hand.

"Eli," I reply, shaking her hand.

For a moment, we just stand there, the music swirling around us, and I feel something shift—like maybe this summer is going to be different. Maybe it's not just about poetry or music or figuring out who I am. Maybe it's about something else entirely.

Jasmine

I don't know what it is about Eli, but something about him feels... steady. Like an anchor in the middle of all this festival chaos. He's not what I expected—quiet, a little shy, but there's something in his eyes that makes me want to keep talking to him. Something thoughtful.

"So, what brings you to the festival?" I ask, trying to keep the conversation going as we walk through the crowd.

He shrugs, glancing around at the stages and the booths. "I love music. And poetry. There's something about the way the two blend together here, you know?"

I nod, understanding exactly what he means. "Yeah. Music's always been my thing. But I've been thinking about blending it with my photography somehow. I don't know, like capturing the stories behind the songs."

Eli's face lights up a little, like he gets it. "That's really cool. It's like... finding the poetry in the pictures."

"Exactly," I say, surprised at how easy it is to talk to him. He's not like most guys I've met—there's a softness to him, an openness that makes me want to share more than I usually would.

We keep walking, the conversation flowing effortlessly. We talk about music, about art, and I find myself opening up in a way I didn't expect. He tells me about his love of bluegrass, and I share stories about how I'm exploring my Chinese heritage through my photography. It's... nice. Comfortable.

As we pass one of the smaller stages, the band starts playing a familiar bluegrass tune, and I feel myself relax into the rhythm of the music. This is what I love about Maplewood Grove—there's always a song in the air, always a sense of community and connection.

I glance at Eli, and for a second, I wonder if maybe—just maybe —this summer is about more than finding my voice through music and photography.

Maybe it's about finding something else, too.

Chapter Two

JASMINE

I can feel the energy of the festival humming all around me, like a pulse in the air. There's something about Maplewood Grove during the Folk Music Festival that makes everything feel more alive. It's the music, the laughter, the mingling of people from all walks of life. It's one of those rare moments where time feels like it's standing still.

"Are you ready?" Rosa asks, her eyes bright with excitement as we weave through the crowd, making our way to the stage where I'm set to perform in less than an hour.

I nod, though my heart is racing. "As ready as I'll ever be."

This is my first time performing at the festival—something I've been dreaming about since I was a kid, watching the musicians on stage with their guitars, banjos, and harmonicas, their music filling the warm summer air. Now it's my turn, and that thought is both exhilarating and terrifying.

The main stage is alive with sound. A local band is playing a fast-paced bluegrass tune, and I can't help but tap my foot along to the beat. The lead singer's voice is raw and gritty, but full of soul, and the way the audience responds to him makes me even more nervous.

That's the kind of connection I want with the crowd—a moment where it's not just about the music but about feeling something.

"Hey, there's Eli," Rosa says, nodding toward the other side of the crowd. I follow her gaze and spot him standing near the back, notebook in hand, his eyes fixed on the stage.

I smile, a little flutter of nerves settling in my chest. Eli's different. There's something about him that feels... familiar, like he's always been a part of this town, a part of the music. Even though we just met, talking to him feels like slipping into an easy rhythm, like a song I've known all my life.

I glance back at Rosa. "I'm going to say hi."

She grins. "Go for it. I'll be right here."

I weave through the crowd, my heart picking up speed with every step. When I reach him, he's so focused on the music that he doesn't notice me right away. I tap his shoulder lightly.

He turns, his eyes widening with surprise. "Oh, hey, Jasmine."

"Hey," I say, feeling a little breathless for reasons I can't quite explain. "What are you writing?"

He holds up his notebook, looking a little shy. "Just some thoughts. I like writing during live performances—it helps me capture the feeling of the music."

"That's cool," I say, glancing at the messy scrawl of his notes. "You're a poet, right?"

He nods. "Yeah. I've been writing for a while. I'm not sure where it's going, but it's how I make sense of things."

I smile at that. "I get it. Music's like that for me too."

He looks at me, his expression thoughtful. "Are you nervous about your set?"

"A little," I admit. "It's my first time performing at the festival."

"You'll be great," he says, his voice soft but sure. "I can tell."

Something about the way he says it makes the knots in my stomach loosen. I don't know why, but I believe him.

Eli

I didn't expect to meet someone like Jasmine at the festival. I didn't expect to meet anyone, really. I came here for the music, for the poetry, for the quiet moments in between. But now, with Jasmine standing in front of me, it's like everything else fades into the background.

Her presence is magnetic. She has this energy that draws people in, this confidence that makes you want to know more. But there's something else too—something softer, something vulnerable that she hides just beneath the surface. And I'm curious. I want to understand what makes her tick, what drives her.

"You play guitar, right?" I ask, glancing at the instrument case slung over her shoulder.

She nods, shifting the strap a little. "Yeah. I've been playing for a few years. My parents weren't exactly thrilled about it at first, but music's always been my thing."

I raise an eyebrow. "Not thrilled? How could they not be?"

She laughs, though there's a touch of something sad in the sound. "They had other plans for me. More... traditional plans. But I've always been the black sheep in the family."

I nod, understanding that feeling all too well. I've always been the quiet one, the one who'd rather bury his nose in a book than deal with the real world. My parents didn't always get it, but they've come around. Maybe Jasmine's parents will too.

Before I can say anything else, a voice comes over the speakers, announcing her set. Jasmine glances at me, her nerves flashing in her eyes for a split second before she steels herself. "Wish me luck?"

"You don't need it," I say, trying to sound more confident than I feel. "But good luck anyway."

She smiles—really smiles—and it hits me like a punch to the gut.

There's something about that smile that makes me want to hold onto it, to make sure she never loses it.

I watch as she makes her way to the stage, guitar in hand, and I find myself holding my breath as she steps up to the mic. The crowd is buzzing, the air thick with anticipation. But Jasmine? She looks like she's exactly where she's supposed to be.

She strums the first chord, and the sound ripples through the audience like a wave. It's soft at first, gentle, but then her voice comes in—low and smooth, with just the right amount of grit—and I feel it. The connection. The music wraps around me like a poem, every word, every note, pulling me in deeper.

I don't know how long I stand there, listening, but by the time her set is over, the crowd is roaring with applause. And I'm standing there, stunned, because I know I've just witnessed something special.

Jasmine steps off the stage, her eyes scanning the crowd, and when she spots me, there's this look in her eyes—this mix of excitement and relief—that makes my chest tighten.

"You were amazing," I say as soon as she reaches me.

She shrugs, trying to play it cool, but I can see the pride in her eyes. "Thanks."

And just like that, I know. I know that this summer—this festival—it's going to be different. Because Jasmine Turner is something different. Something... more.

Jasmine

I've never been great at accepting compliments, especially after a performance. There's always that little voice in the back of my head telling me I could've done better, that I didn't hit the right note or that the timing was off. But when Eli tells me I was amazing, I can't help but believe him.

There's something in the way he says it—like he's not just talking about the music, but about me. And I don't know how to feel about that.

"So, what did you think?" I ask, trying to keep my tone light as we start walking away from the stage.

Eli glances at me, his eyes thoughtful. "I think you're talented. Like, really talented."

I laugh, feeling a blush creep up my neck. "Thanks. I mean, it wasn't perfect, but—"

"It was," he interrupts, his voice quiet but firm. "It was perfect."

My heart skips a beat at the intensity in his eyes, and for a moment, I forget how to breathe. No one's ever looked at me like that before—like they see all of me, the good and the bad, and they still think I'm... worth something.

I clear my throat, trying to shake off the feeling. "So, what about you? You're into poetry, right?"

He nods, pulling his notebook out of his back pocket. "Yeah. I've been writing for a while now. It helps me... I don't know... figure things out."

"I get that," I say, glancing at the scrawl of words on the page. "I think music's the same for me. It's like... I can express things I don't know how to say otherwise."

Eli nods, and there's this moment between us—this quiet understanding that I don't think I've ever had with anyone before. It's like we're speaking the same language, even though we're using different words.

As we walk through the festival, the music fading into the background, I can't help but feel something shift. There's this pull between us, this attraction that I'm not sure how to navigate. It's exciting and terrifying all at once.

But for the first time, I'm not running away from it. I'm letting it happen, letting myself feel it.

And I think... I think I'm okay with that.

Chapter Three

Eli

I've always been the guy on the outside looking in. In high school, I was the quiet kid with his nose in a book, the one who watched life happen but never really felt part of it. But standing here next to Jasmine, listening to the buzz of the festival around us, I feel like maybe—just maybe—that's starting to change.

We've been spending the afternoon wandering around the festival, catching bits of different performances and stopping to talk to some of the musicians. Jasmine lights up every time we pass by a guitar or a banjo, her fingers itching to play, even when she's not holding her own instrument. It's like music is a part of her, woven into every smile, every laugh, every word.

"So, you never told me—what made you get into music?" I ask as we sit down by one of the smaller stages, where a fiddler is playing a soft, mournful tune.

Jasmine pauses, tilting her head as she thinks. "It's hard to say. I guess it's always been there, you know? My parents had this old record player, and I used to sit in front of it for hours, just listening to whatever they played. Mostly Chinese ballads, but I'd find other records too. Bluegrass, rock, folk music... I was obsessed with the stories behind the songs."

"That's cool," I say, leaning forward, my elbows resting on my knees. "You ever think about blending that with your photography? Like, telling stories through both music and pictures?"

Her eyes brighten, and she looks at me like I've just said something brilliant. "I've actually thought about that. It's part of what I want to do eventually—merge the two somehow. But I haven't figured out how yet."

"Maybe you don't have to figure it all out at once," I suggest, watching her carefully. "Maybe you can just let it happen."

She smiles, but there's a hint of uncertainty in it. "Yeah. Maybe."

There's a pause, the music from the stage filling the silence between us. I'm not sure if I should push further or let it go, but something tells me that Jasmine doesn't open up easily. She's like me in that way—quiet, thoughtful, always holding something back.

I reach into my back pocket, pulling out my notebook. "You ever write down your ideas? Like, just put them on paper, even if you don't know what they mean yet?"

Jasmine raises an eyebrow, her lips quirking in amusement. "You mean like a journal?"

"Kind of," I say, flipping through the pages. "I write down poems, but a lot of them don't make sense at first. It's just pieces of thoughts, stuff I'm trying to figure out. Sometimes the meaning comes later."

She looks at me, her eyes softening, like she understands exactly what I'm saying. "That's a good idea," she murmurs, her voice thoughtful. "Maybe I'll try that."

I smile, feeling like I've given her something—even if it's just a small nudge in the right direction.

Jasmine

Maplewood Grove always feels like it's holding its breath, waiting for something to happen. It's a small town where everyone knows everyone else's business, where the same people show up at every event and the same conversations happen at every town meeting. But during the Folk Music Festival, the town comes alive.

I've never really been a part of it before. Not like this.

"Everyone here is so... invested," I say as Eli and I walk past a group of volunteers setting up booths for the next performance. "I mean, I knew the festival was a big deal, but I didn't realize how much the whole town gets involved."

Eli nods, glancing around at the bustling scene. "Yeah, that's Maplewood Grove for you. It's small, but when something happens, it's like the whole town shows up."

I laugh, nodding in agreement. "I guess that's part of the charm, huh?"

"Definitely," he says, his gaze lingering on the stage where a local band is setting up for their set. "I think that's why I've always liked it here. There's this sense of community, even when you feel like you're on the outside."

I glance at him, curious. "You ever feel like you don't fit in here?"

Eli shrugs, his hands slipping into his pockets. "Sometimes. I mean, it's a small town, and I'm more of an introvert. But the people here... they're good. Even when they don't always get me."

I nod, understanding more than I thought I would. I've always felt like the odd one out in my family—my parents were all about tradition, and I've always been the one pushing against that, trying to figure out where I fit.

"Yeah, I get that," I say, my voice quiet. "I love this town, but sometimes it feels... too small. Like I need to get out, see the world, do something bigger."

Eli looks at me, his eyes thoughtful. "But you still come back."

I smile softly. "Yeah. I guess I do."

The music starts, and we both fall silent, the sound of guitars and fiddles filling the air. I glance around at the crowd—at the familiar faces, the laughter, the music—and for the first time in a long time, I feel like I'm a part of something bigger than myself.

Eli

There's something about Jasmine that pulls people in.

As the festival rolls on, I notice it more and more. The way the musicians talk to her like they've known her for years, the way the other performers nod in her direction, like they're acknowledging one of their own. And it's not just because she's a great musician. It's because she's one of those people who's genuinely interested in what everyone else is doing. She listens. She cares.

"I think you've got a fan club," I tease as we make our way through the festival grounds, nodding toward a group of local artists who wave at her as we pass by.

Jasmine laughs, shrugging. "Nah, they're just being nice."

"I don't think it's just that," I say, watching her closely. "People like you. They respect you."

Her smile falters for a moment, and I catch a glimpse of something vulnerable in her eyes. "I don't know about that. I've always felt like I'm just... figuring things out. Like everyone else knows what they're doing, and I'm just faking it."

I stop walking, turning to face her. "You're not faking it, Jasmine. You're talented. And people see that. They respect you because you're good at what you do."

She looks at me, her expression softening, and for a moment, I can see the uncertainty she hides so well. "Thanks," she murmurs, her voice barely audible over the sound of the festival.

I smile, feeling a warmth spread through my chest. "Anytime."

We continue walking, the sounds of the festival fading into the background as we make our way toward the riverbank. It's quieter here, away from the main stage, and I feel like I can finally catch my breath.

"Sometimes I feel like I don't belong here either," Jasmine says after a long pause, her voice quiet and thoughtful. "Like I'm supposed to be somewhere else, doing something bigger."

I nod, understanding exactly what she means. "Yeah. But maybe you can do both. Maybe you can be part of this community and still find a way to do something bigger."

She looks at me, her eyes searching mine for a moment. "Maybe."

And in that moment, I realize something. Maybe this summer isn't just about figuring out who I am or what I want. Maybe it's about helping Jasmine figure that out too.

Chapter Four

JASMINE

Everything was going perfectly.

I've spent the past week riding a high from the festival—the music, the performances, the community... and Eli. We've been spending more time together, walking around the festival grounds, catching different shows, talking about life and art and everything in between. I didn't expect to meet someone like him, someone who just *gets* me, but here we are.

Now I'm standing backstage, guitar in hand, waiting for my turn to perform at one of the festival's smaller stages. I've been practicing for this set all week, picking out the perfect songs, rehearsing until my fingers were sore. I was ready.

But then everything went wrong.

There's a problem with the sound system—something about faulty wiring or blown speakers—and the whole performance is canceled. Just like that. No warning, no explanation, just a hurried apology from the stage manager and a promise that they'll reschedule... eventually.

I stand there, stunned, as the other performers shuffle off the stage, disappointment written across their faces. The crowd starts to disperse, murmurs of confusion and frustration filling the air.

This was supposed to be my moment.

I feel a knot form in my throat, and before I know it, I'm storming off, desperate to get away from the stage, from the crowd, from everything. I push through the festival grounds, past the vendors and musicians, until I find a quiet spot by the riverbank, far from the noise and the people.

I drop down onto the grass, hugging my guitar case to my chest as tears prick the corners of my eyes. I hate this feeling—this sense of helplessness, like everything I've worked for is slipping through my fingers.

I hear footsteps approaching, but I don't look up. I already know who it is.

"Jasmine?"

Eli's voice is soft, cautious, like he's not sure if he should be here. I keep my eyes trained on the water, blinking back the tears.

"They canceled my set," I say, my voice flat. "The sound system broke, and they canceled the whole thing."

Eli sits down next to me, close enough that I can feel the warmth of him, but he doesn't say anything right away. He just... sits. And for some reason, that makes it a little easier to breathe.

"I'm sorry," he says after a moment, his voice low. "That sucks."

I nod, not trusting myself to speak.

"I know how much this meant to you," he adds, glancing over at me. "You've been working so hard for this."

I let out a shaky breath, my hands tightening around the handle of my guitar case. "It's just... I thought this was it. My chance to show what I can do, to prove that I'm good enough. And now it's gone."

Eli watches me, his eyes thoughtful. "It's not gone. It's just... delayed. You'll get another chance."

I shake my head, frustration bubbling up inside me. "You don't get it, Eli. This was supposed to be *my moment*. And now I feel like... I don't know. Like I'm never going to be enough. Not for music, not for my parents, not for... anything."

The words spill out before I can stop them, and once they're out, I feel this strange sense of relief. Like I've been holding them in for too long.

Eli doesn't flinch. He doesn't tell me I'm being dramatic or that I should just get over it. He just looks at me, his expression soft and understanding. "I get it," he says quietly. "More than you think."

Eli

I didn't realize how much Jasmine was holding back.

I've seen her in her element—on stage, in the crowd, surrounded by music and people who love her. She's confident, sure of herself, always in control. But here, by the river, she's... vulnerable. She's real. And it makes me want to protect her, to be there for her, even if I don't have all the answers.

"I know what it feels like," I say, my voice steady, even though my heart is racing. "To feel like you're not enough. To feel like no matter what you do, it's never good enough. But you are enough, Jasmine. You're more than enough."

She looks at me, her eyes filled with doubt, and I can see how much she's struggling to believe that. I get it. I've been there. I'm still there, most days.

"I've always felt like I'm on the outside," I continue, my gaze drifting toward the river. "Like I'm not quite... part of everything. I love poetry, but sometimes I wonder if I'm wasting my time. If it even matters."

Jasmine frowns, her brow furrowing. "But your poetry is beautiful, Eli. You have a gift."

I smile softly, my heart warming at her words. "So do you. And just because something didn't go the way you planned doesn't mean it's not going to happen. You'll find another way. I know you will."

For a moment, she doesn't say anything, just looks at me like she's trying to figure me out. And then, slowly, she nods. "I guess I've always had this idea that everything has to go perfectly, or it's a failure. But maybe you're right. Maybe I can find another way."

"You will," I say, my voice firm. "And when you do, it'll be even better."

Jasmine lets out a small laugh, her eyes softening. "How do you always know the right thing to say?"

I shrug, feeling a blush creep up my neck. "I don't. I'm just... being honest."

She smiles at that, and for the first time since we sat down, she looks lighter. Like the weight of the disappointment is starting to lift.

"Thank you, Eli," she says, her voice quiet. "I don't know what I would've done without you here."

I smile, feeling a warmth spread through my chest. "Anytime."

Jasmine

The sun is starting to dip below the horizon, casting a soft, golden light over the river. The water glitters, reflecting the fading sunlight, and for a moment, everything feels... still. Peaceful. Like the world is giving me permission to slow down and just breathe.

I glance over at Eli, who's sitting beside me, staring out at the water with that thoughtful expression I'm starting to recognize. He's quiet, but it's not an awkward silence. It's comfortable, like we don't need words to fill the space between us.

"I've never really talked to anyone about this stuff before," I admit, my voice barely more than a whisper. "About how much I want music to work out. About how scared I am that it won't."

Eli looks at me, his expression soft but serious. "Why not?"

I shrug, my fingers tracing the edge of my guitar case. "I don't know. I guess I've always felt like I had to be strong, like I couldn't let anyone see that I'm scared. But with you... it's different. I feel like I can be honest."

He smiles, and there's something in his eyes that makes my heart skip a beat. "You don't have to be strong all the time, Jasmine. It's okay to be scared. It's okay to not have it all figured out."

I let out a small laugh, shaking my head. "I feel like you've got it all figured out, though."

He laughs too, shaking his head. "Trust me, I don't. I'm just as lost as you are."

We sit there for a while, the sounds of the festival fading into the distance as the night settles in around us. It's quiet here by the river, and for the first time in a long time, I feel... at peace. Like maybe I don't have to have it all figured out right now. Like maybe it's okay to just... be.

Eli reaches over, gently placing his hand on top of mine. The gesture is small, but it sends a wave of warmth through me, and I find myself leaning into the moment, letting the quiet comfort of it wrap around me.

"I'm glad I met you," I say softly, my heart pounding in my chest.

Eli squeezes my hand, his voice just as quiet. "Me too."

And in that moment, by the river, I know that everything is going to be okay.

Chapter Five

JASMINE

The rest of the festival feels different now. Not the music, not the energy—that's still as vibrant as ever—but something has shifted between me and Eli. It's like the air around us is charged with something new, something I'm not sure I'm ready to name yet.

We've spent the past few days practically glued to each other's side, bouncing between performances and quiet moments by the river. It's easy being around him, like we've known each other forever. He gets me in a way no one else has, and I don't have to pretend around him. I can just be... me.

But with every passing moment, I can feel the weight of something building—something more than friendship. And it terrifies me.

"You okay?" Eli asks, nudging me with his elbow as we sit on the grass, watching a local bluegrass band play. His voice is soft, thoughtful, as if he's worried I've drifted too far away in my own head.

I glance at him, offering a small smile. "Yeah, I'm fine. Just... thinking."

"About?"

I hesitate, chewing on my bottom lip. You. Us. Whatever this is between us. But I can't bring myself to say it. Not yet. "About what happens after the festival."

Eli's expression softens, and he leans back on his elbows, looking up at the sky. "Yeah. I've been thinking about that too."

I don't know what I was expecting him to say, but something about the way he says it makes my chest tighten. He's been thinking about it too. So... I'm not the only one.

But what does that mean?

The band finishes their set, and the crowd bursts into applause. I clap along, but my mind is racing. What does this mean? What happens after the music stops?

Eli

I've been trying to play it cool, but I can feel it too. There's something happening between me and Jasmine—something I didn't expect. It's more than just friendship, more than just a connection over music and poetry. It's... something else.

And it scares the hell out of me.

I've never been great at relationships. I'm the guy who lives in his head, who spends more time with his notebook than with actual people. But Jasmine? She's different. Being around her makes me feel like maybe I don't have to have it all figured out. Like maybe I can just let things happen.

But I can also tell she's holding back. There's this hesitation in her eyes, this tension in her body whenever we get too close—like she's afraid of what might happen if we actually *talk* about what's going on between us.

"Hey," I say, my voice low as I shift closer to her. "You sure you're okay? You seem... distant."

She glances at me, her lips pressing into a thin line. "I'm just thinking about... stuff. The future."

I nod, even though I don't really know what she means. Is she thinking about us? Or is it something else?

Before I can ask, she stands up, brushing the grass off her jeans. "I'm going to grab a drink. You want anything?"

I shake my head, watching as she walks away, her shoulders tense. I don't know what's going on in her head, but I can feel her pulling back, and I don't know how to stop it.

***

Jasmine

I need space. I need to clear my head.

As I make my way to one of the food trucks, I catch sight of Eli talking to someone—a guy I don't recognize, but he looks familiar in that *small-town, everyone-knows-everyone* way. Eli's expression is serious, his hands gesturing as he talks. I can't hear what they're saying over the hum of the festival, but something about the way Eli's face is set makes my heart sink.

Curiosity tugs at me, and before I realize what I'm doing, I slow my steps, trying to catch bits of their conversation.

"...just don't know if I'm staying here," I hear Eli say, his voice quieter than usual but heavy with something I can't quite place. "I mean, this is all great, but..."

He trails off, shaking his head, and the guy he's talking to claps him on the back with a knowing smile.

My stomach twists. Is he talking about leaving?

For the first time, I feel like the ground beneath me isn't as solid as I thought. This whole week, I've been trying to figure out what's happening between us, what it means, and now... now I'm not even sure if Eli's staying in Maplewood Grove. If he's planning on sticking around or if this—whatever *this* is—was just temporary.

I turn away before I can hear any more, my heart pounding in my chest. I shouldn't care. I shouldn't be so affected by this. But I am. And that realization scares me more than anything.

Eli

Something's wrong. I can feel it the moment Jasmine comes back with her drink. She's distant, her smile doesn't quite reach her eyes, and she's not making eye contact like she usually does.

I try to shake off the nagging feeling in my gut, but it's hard to ignore. "You okay?" I ask, glancing at her as she takes a sip from her drink.

She nods, but it's a quick, almost dismissive nod. "Yeah, I'm fine."

Fine. The universal word for *I'm definitely not fine but I don't want to talk about it.*

I wait for her to say more, to explain what's bothering her, but she doesn't. She just turns her attention back to the stage, pretending to be interested in the next performance.

I don't push, but it feels like there's a wall between us now, one that wasn't there before. It's frustrating because things were going so well. We were finally getting closer, finally starting to understand each other. But now... now she's shutting me out.

And I don't know why.

Jasmine

I've spent the rest of the day avoiding Eli. Every time I see him, I feel this pit in my stomach, this gnawing feeling that whatever's been happening between us is already slipping away. I don't know why it bothers me so much—after all, we've only known each other for a week—but it does.

I can't stop thinking about what he said. About how he's not sure if he's staying in Maplewood Grove. It shouldn't be a big deal, but it feels like one. Like I've been building something in my head, and now it's crumbling before it even had a chance to take shape.

I shake my head, trying to push the thoughts away as I focus on the music. But even the familiar twang of the banjo and the steady rhythm of the bass can't distract me from the ache in my chest.

I don't know what to do.

All I know is that I need to put some distance between me and Eli. I need to protect myself before I get hurt.

Chapter Six

JASMINE

I've been avoiding Eli for the past couple of days, but it's only made me feel worse. I can't shake the pit in my stomach, the nagging feeling that I've misunderstood something important. But every time I see him, every time I think about what he said, it feels like there's this wall between us that I can't break down.

So now, instead of dealing with it, I'm hiding out in the back of the Whispering Willow, pretending to work on the store's social media. The festival is still in full swing, and the café is buzzing with people grabbing coffee between sets, but my mind is a million miles away.

I scroll through photos on my camera, but none of them hold my attention. I can't stop thinking about Eli—about how close we were getting, how easy it was to talk to him, and how quickly it all slipped away.

I sigh, dropping my head into my hands. Why am I like this? Why can't I just ask him what he meant?

"Jasmine?"

I freeze, my heart skipping a beat at the sound of Eli's voice.

Slowly, I lift my head, and there he is, standing at the counter, his expression soft but concerned.

"Hey," I say, my voice barely above a whisper.

He steps closer, hesitating for a moment before sitting down across from me. "You've been... distant. Did I do something?"

I bite my lip, my fingers tightening around my camera. Part of me wants to run, to avoid this conversation altogether, but I know I can't keep doing that. I need to face this.

"I overheard you talking to someone at the festival," I say quietly, my heart pounding in my chest. "You said you weren't sure if you were staying in Maplewood Grove. I just... I thought we were starting to... I don't know... connect. And if you're leaving..."

Eli's eyes widen, realization dawning on his face. "Wait, you heard that?"

I nod, feeling foolish for not just asking him sooner.

He lets out a long breath, leaning back in his chair. "Jasmine, I wasn't talking about leaving *you*. I was talking about college—about whether I'm staying at the local community college or transferring to a school out of state. I haven't decided yet."

My chest tightens as his words sink in. College. Not leaving Maplewood Grove. Not leaving me.

I stare at him, my emotions swirling, a mix of relief and embarrassment flooding through me. "I thought... I don't know what I thought."

Eli leans forward, his eyes filled with concern. "Jasmine, I'm not going anywhere. I don't know what's going to happen with school, but that doesn't mean I'm just going to disappear."

I look down, guilt gnawing at me. "I guess I jumped to conclusions."

He shakes his head, his voice soft. "No, I get it. I've been thinking a lot about my future too, and it's... scary. I don't know where I'm headed, but I know I want to be here. With you."

Eli

I've never been good at this—at talking about feelings, at being vulnerable. But sitting across from Jasmine, watching the way her shoulders tense, the way her eyes flicker with uncertainty, I know I have to try. I can't let her pull away from me. Not now.

"I'm sorry I didn't say anything earlier," I continue, my voice low. "I should've told you what was going on, but I didn't want to make things complicated."

She looks up at me, her eyes softening. "It's not just about the college thing, though, is it? It's about... us."

I swallow hard, nodding. "Yeah. It's about us."

There's a long pause as we both sit there, the weight of what we haven't said hanging in the air between us. I can feel my heart pounding in my chest, the fear creeping up my spine. But I can't hide from this anymore. Not if I want things to work with her.

"I've never been good at relationships," I admit, my voice shaking slightly. "I've always felt like I'm on the outside, like I don't really fit anywhere. But with you... I don't feel like that. You make me feel like I belong."

Jasmine's breath catches, and I see something shift in her expression. She's not just hearing my words—she's feeling them. I can tell because it's the same way I feel when she talks about her music, about her dreams. We're both chasing something, both trying to figure out where we fit in this world.

"I've been scared too," she says softly, her fingers tracing the edge of her camera. "I've spent so much time trying to prove that I'm good enough—that my music, my photography, that *I* am enough. And when I thought you might leave... I panicked."

I nod, understanding completely. "You don't have to prove anything to me, Jasmine. You're more than enough."

She looks up at me, her eyes wide, and for a moment, neither of us says anything. We just sit there, letting the words sink in, letting the truth of what we've both been avoiding finally settle between us.

Jasmine

I don't know when it happened, but somewhere between the quiet conversations and the music-filled nights, I realized that I care about Eli. Really care. And it scares me because I've never let myself feel this way about anyone before. But sitting here, hearing him say those words, knowing he's just as scared as I am... it makes me want to stop running.

"I'm sorry I pulled away," I say softly, meeting his gaze. "I just... I've been scared of letting someone in. But I don't want to do that anymore."

Eli's eyes soften, and he reaches across the table, gently taking my hand in his. "You don't have to be scared, Jasmine. We can figure this out together."

I nod, feeling a sense of relief wash over me. For the first time in a long time, I feel like I'm not alone. I'm not navigating this uncertain future by myself. Eli's here, and he wants to be a part of it.

"So, where do we go from here?" I ask, my voice steady but hopeful.

Eli smiles, and it's the kind of smile that makes my heart skip a beat. "How about we take it one step at a time?"

Eli

I can't stop smiling. I know we've still got a lot to figure out, but the weight that's been hanging over me for the past few days is finally gone. Jasmine and I are okay. We're more than okay.

"Actually," I say, leaning forward, a grin spreading across my face. "I have an idea for our next step."

Jasmine raises an eyebrow, intrigued. "Oh yeah?"

"There's an open mic night at the festival tonight," I explain, my heart racing with excitement. "I was thinking... maybe we could perform together."

Her eyes widen, surprise flashing across her face. "Together? Like a duet?"

I nod, feeling a thrill of anticipation. "Yeah. You on guitar, me reading one of my poems... I think we'd make a pretty good team."

Jasmine hesitates for a moment, but then her lips curl into a smile, and I know she's in. "You know what? That sounds amazing."

I grin, my heart pounding with excitement. "Great. Let's do it."

Jasmine

Later that night, as the festival winds down and the open mic night begins, Eli and I stand backstage, waiting for our turn. I can feel the familiar rush of nerves in my stomach, but this time it's different. This time, I'm not doing it alone.

Eli stands beside me, his notebook in hand, and when he glances at me, his eyes filled with quiet confidence, I feel a sense of calm settle over me. We're in this together.

When our names are called, we step onto the stage, and I take a deep breath, strumming the first chord on my guitar. The crowd quiets, and for a moment, it's just me and Eli, the music and the words weaving together like they were always meant to.

Eli's voice is soft but sure as he recites his poem, the rhythm of his words syncing perfectly with the melody I'm playing. And as I listen, I realize something: this is what I've been searching for. Not just the music, not just the photography, but the connection—the feeling of being part of something bigger than myself.

As the last note fades, the crowd bursts into applause, and I glance over at Eli, my heart swelling with gratitude. For him. For us. For everything.

We step off the stage, and before I can say anything, Eli pulls me into a hug, his arms wrapping around me like I'm exactly where I'm supposed to be.

"You were amazing," he whispers, his breath warm against my ear.

"So were you," I whisper back, my heart pounding in my chest.

And in that moment, I know that we're going to be okay. Whatever happens next, whatever the future holds, we'll face it together.

Chapter Seven

JASMINE

The night air is crisp, the festival winding down after a long, magical summer. I'm still riding the high from our performance at the open mic—something about standing on that stage with Eli, sharing our music and words, felt... right. Like all the pieces finally fell into place.

We're walking hand in hand through the festival grounds, the quiet hum of conversations and distant music filling the air. Lanterns line the pathways, casting a soft, golden glow over everything, making the town look like something out of a dream.

"I still can't believe we did that," I say, squeezing Eli's hand. "I never thought I'd perform a duet. Especially not with poetry."

He chuckles, his thumb brushing over the back of my hand. "You sounded amazing, Jasmine. It was like the music and the words were made for each other."

I smile, feeling my cheeks warm. "It felt... different. Like we were creating something bigger than just a song or a poem."

"Exactly," Eli says, his voice soft but full of meaning. "That's what it's all about. Creating something together."

I glance at him, my heart skipping a beat. There's something about the way he's looking at me—like he's been waiting to say something, but he's not sure how to start.

"Jasmine," he begins, his voice low. "I know we've been taking things slow, and I don't want to rush you, but... I need you to know something."

I swallow hard, my heart pounding in my chest. Here it comes.

He stops walking, turning to face me, his eyes searching mine. "I love you."

The words hang in the air between us, heavy with meaning, and for a moment, I can't breathe. I wasn't expecting this—wasn't expecting to feel this way so soon. But as I look at him, standing there with his heart wide open, I realize something. I love him too.

"I love you, Eli," I whisper, the words coming easier than I thought they would.

A slow smile spreads across his face, and before I know it, he's pulling me into his arms, his lips brushing mine in a soft, tender kiss. It's not the kind of kiss that sets off fireworks or makes the world spin —it's the kind that makes everything feel steady, like I'm exactly where I'm supposed to be.

When we finally pull apart, Eli rests his forehead against mine, his voice barely more than a whisper. "I've been waiting to say that for a while now."

I laugh softly, my heart feeling lighter than it has in weeks. "Me too."

Eli

I can't stop smiling. I didn't think I'd ever get to this point—to the moment where I could actually say the words out loud, to admit to myself and to Jasmine how much she means to me. But now that it's out there, it feels like everything else is falling into place.

We're still standing close, her hands in mine, and I can feel the warmth of her breath on my skin. There's this sense of peace that settles over me, like the chaos of the last few days doesn't matter anymore. Because she's here. And she loves me.

"You want to head back to the stage?" I ask, nodding toward where the last performers of the festival are wrapping up their set.

Jasmine grins. "Are you suggesting another duet?"

I shrug, trying to play it cool. "Maybe. If you're up for it."

She laughs, shaking her head. "I can't say no to that."

We make our way back to the main stage, the crowd thinning out as the night comes to a close. It's quieter now, more intimate, and when we step up to the stage, it feels like we're the only two people in the world.

Jasmine picks up her guitar, strumming a soft melody, and I pull out my notebook, flipping to one of my favorite poems. The words come easily, flowing with the rhythm of her music, and for the first time, I feel like I'm exactly where I'm supposed to be—like everything I've been searching for has led me here, to this moment with her.

The crowd watches in silence, their attention focused on us, but it's not about them anymore. It's about us. About the music. About the connection we've built over these past few weeks.

As the last note fades, the audience bursts into applause, and Jasmine turns to me, her eyes bright with excitement. "That was amazing."

I grin, my heart pounding. "We make a pretty good team."

Jasmine

The crowd is still clapping, but all I can focus on is Eli—on the way his eyes light up when he smiles, on the way his hand feels in mine. For the first time in a long time, I feel like I'm exactly where

I'm supposed to be. No more running, no more second-guessing. Just this. Just him.

As the applause dies down, I glance out at the crowd, recognizing a few familiar faces. Rosa is grinning at me from the front row, giving me a thumbs-up. Mr. Stevens is nodding approvingly, looking proud. And scattered throughout the audience are other people from town —people who have seen me grow up, who have watched me struggle to find my place.

And now, standing on this stage with Eli, I finally feel like I've found it.

I glance at Eli, and he gives me a small nod, as if to say, *Go for it.* So I do.

"I just want to say thank you," I begin, my voice steady despite the butterflies in my stomach. "This festival means so much to me— to both of us. It's been a chance to share our music, to connect with the community, and to find something we didn't expect."

I pause, glancing at Eli, and he squeezes my hand.

"We've spent the past few weeks figuring things out—figuring out who we are, what we want. And I think I speak for both of us when I say... we've found something special here. Something worth holding onto."

The crowd breaks into applause again, and I smile, feeling a warmth spread through me. This is it. This is where I belong.

Eli

After the applause fades, Jasmine and I step off the stage, hand in hand, and make our way back into the crowd. The festival is coming to an end, but there's still this buzz in the air, this feeling of excitement and celebration that makes everything feel electric.

People stop us as we walk, congratulating us on our performance, offering kind words and smiles. It's strange, being in the spotlight like this, but with Jasmine by my side, it feels... good. Like we're a part of something bigger than ourselves.

I glance over at the other couples who have gathered in the square —familiar faces from around town, people we've seen throughout the festival. There's this sense of unity, of connection, that wasn't there before. It's like the festival has brought us all closer, reminding us of what matters most: love, community, and the bonds we build with each other.

I can see Gene and Betty Lou laughing together by one of the food trucks, sharing a plate of fries and bickering like an old married couple. Across the way, I spot Isabel and Richard, hand in hand as they watch their daughter dance to the music still playing from one of the stages.

It's like everything is coming full circle—like all the stories we've been a part of, all the people we've connected with, are finding their own happy endings.

Jasmine

As the night winds down, Eli and I find ourselves back at the riverbank where we've spent so much time together over the past few weeks. The stars are out, reflecting on the water, and there's a quiet peace in the air that makes everything feel... perfect.

We sit down on the grass, leaning against each other, and for a moment, we just breathe in the stillness.

"What do you think happens next?" Eli asks, his voice soft.

I smile, my heart swelling with hope and excitement. "I don't know. But whatever it is, we'll figure it out."

He grins, pressing a kiss to my forehead. "One step at a time, right?"

"One step at a time," I agree, resting my head on his shoulder.

And as we sit there, watching the stars and listening to the distant hum of the festival, I know that this is just the beginning. The beginning of something beautiful, something real.

Something that's ours.

The End
Did you enjoy Small Town Memories?
Consider reviewing it on Goodreads, Bookbub, or your favorite retailer. Reviews help me reach new readers.

Read **Small Town Miracles**, the next collection in the **Maplewood Grove** series!

Get this FREE Maplewood Story when you join my newsletter at www.daisylandishromance.com

Subscriber Exclusive!

About the Author

Daisy Landish is a clean romance and cozy mystery author whose clean and sweet novellas have tugged at readers' heartstrings around the world. When she's not writing love stories, Daisy spends her time reading, hiking at dawn, and riding into the sunset on her horse, Rosebud.

www.daisylandishromance.com

facebook.com/daisylandishromance

x.com/daisy_landish

instagram.com/daisylandishbooks

amazon.com/author/daisylandish

bookbub.com/authors/daisy-landish

goodreads.com/Daisy_Landish

Also by Daisy Landish

Clean Regency Romance

The Lady Series - The Allington Collection

The Lady Series - The Gillingham Collection

The Lady Series - The Blackmore Collection

The Lady Series - The Norrington Collection

Clean Contemporary Romance

Timeline Retreats - Romantic Comedy

Maplewood Grove Series - Small Town Romance

Love on Spruce Island

Second Chance

Cherry Tree Island

The Wedding Trio

Extra Credit

Counting on the Cowboy

Focusing on the Cowboy

Mistletoe Magic

Grounded at Christmas

Cozy Mysteries

Sophie Brooks Mysteries

Jane and Kennedy Daniels Mysteries

Pine Grove Mysteries

Annie Archer Paranormal Mysteries

Wilma Wade Mysteries

Mike and Maddie Mysteries

Mystic Moonhaven Mysteries

Sweater Weather: Cozy Mysteries for Fall

Summer Vibes: Cozy Mysteries for Summer

Let it Snow: Cozy Mysteries for Winter

Spring Break: Cozy Mysteries for Spring

www.ingramcontent.com/pod-product-compliance
Lightning Source LLC
Chambersburg PA
CBHW050413260626
47156CB00003B/990